Kole Black 1

AUTOGRAPH PAGE

The Risk of Chance

Some chances are worth the risk.

Written By

Kole Black

Edited by

Peggy Riley

This book is a work of fiction. All names, characters, places, and incidents are purely fictional. Any resemblance to any actual events, locales or persons, living or dead is coincidental.

All rights reserved, including the right to reproduce this book or portions thereof in any form.

Copyright 2008

Published by *Spaulden Publishing*, Woodbury, Connecticut, 06798

ISBN: 978-0-6152-1505-1

"*Kole Black*" is a registered trademark and may not be used without expressed written consent. Trademark 2006.

Acknowledgements

First, I must to give thanks to you, Yahweh, for you are Alpha & Omega. I am so grateful for everything that you have blessed me with, for every dream that you have allowed. Thank you for always remembering me with your love and kindness. The stars in the sky worship and adore you. And I will praise you until the day I die. Amen.

Second, I want to thank everybody that helped me to make this possible once again, and everybody I didn't get to thank last time.

Sholina "Queen Redd" Penn> I would have never been able to finish this second book without your support & encouragement. Words could not express all the love & gratitude I feel in my heart. You must have been *"Sent From Heaven!"*

To my literary agent, Gillette Goldsmith, thank you so much for all you've done. Here's to the future!

Jeff "Jays-Groove" Jones> Thank you for another amazing book cover and for the incredible photos. You are a true renaissance man, and a "JONES" of all trades.

And thanks to Ms. Afrikia Green-Whitfield for the artist and technical direction.

Anthony "Byiton" Washington> How do you thank somebody that's been a friend, a brother, a protector & a role model? All I can do is say thank you, and hope that our friendship has given you even at least half of what it's given me. You are my brother for life!

Catherine Jenkins-McGee> Thank you for always being such a loyal friend (When true friendship is in such short supply). God bless you & your family, always.

Thanks to my hometown of Cincinnati, Ohio for all the love. I would also like to thank all the bookstores that supported me (Border's, Walden, Brentano's & Joseph Beth Books).

To my "Blue Chip" peeps> "My 2nd Mama"- Mrs. Jackie Jones: I love you, "The Marketing Guru"- John Jenkins, "The Man to the Max"- James Maxwell & family, "The Mastermind"- Josh Leah, Ms. Vickie Thiery, "The Lovely"- Miss Jewelz Burnes, "The sweetest"- Miss Drea Haysbert, & everybody else that supported me that I may have forgotten to mention, THANK YOU!

To *Ken Anderson* of WDBZ-AM. Thank you for your words inspiration & encouragement. Each day I strive to follow in your footsteps.

To my girl, *Tonetta Chester, Author of "Surviving The Darkest Days"*, thank you so much for all your support and for spreading the word about KOLE BLACK through out Miami & Atlanta.

To my screenwriting partner, Brent Bridges> you are an amazing talent. Let's go get rich!!!

Special thanks to *Ms. Janine Nash (Lady-J)* for always welcoming me to "the set" You are a truly beautiful spirit.

I gotta send a shout out to television producer, *John House from NXS-TV*. Y'all are the bomb! And a special thanks to my favorite television host "*Shonda*" for all the love!

Thanks to all the ladies at Twin Towers in Cincinnati, Ohio that supported my first novel "The Chance She Took". A very special thanks to T-Doc, Donna E., Da-Da, Donna, Tonya,

Kim, Danita & Lanisha and everybody on the second floor & you too *De'Aulo* (I didn't forget you, man). And a huge, huge thanks to *"Miss Innocent" aka A.C.* for lending me your beauty on the front cover of this book, couldn't have done it without ya'!

Special thanks to all my friends> My god-sister Felicia Washington, my wonderful neighbor Ms. Benita, Ms. Trina Jones, Erica Washington, my dawg *Milt Jones*, Lovell Fitzpatrick, Jako Wilson, Kevin Jung, *Mr. Sandy Crawford*, Tia Matthews, Cassandra Kindred, The Badd-Girlz (Yvonne Godfrey, Paula Jackson, LaNisha Peeples, Anita, Innocent, Angie & Danita)

Thanks to all the book clubs that supported me in Atlanta, L.A., Philly, Chicago, Miami, Dallas & Cincinnati.

And thanks to all my fans on Myspace & BlackPlanet. I love you madly!

To my babies, Daddy loves you, always!
To all my family, I love you.

And an extra special thanks to everyone at **Spaulden Publishing** (Shannon Bayliss, Christine Myron, Kelly Reynolds, Ashton Becker & Michelle Donnelly) for believing in me and helping to bring my dreams to life.

To my Dad> If I ever managed to become half the man you are, then I would truly have become a man. You are my hero. And I love you.

I dedicate this book to the memory of my mother, *Dorothy-Jean Peterson*. You will forever be inside my heart. I love you, mama!

Here's a glimpse back at

"The Chance She Took"

CHAPTER 25

While being questioned by the police, a special all points bulletin came over the radio. It was in regard to a murder at the Omni Hotel, "the victim was a 27 year old African American female, with California drivers license DJ01478L registered to an Iesha Ellis of Los Angeles." It went on to say that the victim had been badly mutilated and a suspect was wanted for questioning in connection with the murder, 25 years old Evan Chance of Chicago, Illinois. The suspect was described as an African American male, about 6'1" in height, 185 pounds, with dark brown skin, bald headed, no facial hair, with a slim to muscular build. Approach with caution!"

The detective turned his eyes slowly toward me. "Miss Davis didn't you say that your boyfriends name was Chance, Evan Chance?" He asked.

My heart began to pound against my chest like a sledgehammer as sweat poured from my brow. "Yes! But he is not a murderer! He could never do anything like this! You need to be out there lookin' for the mutha'fuckas that did this to me, you find them and I bet you'll find Iesha's killer. Chance did not do this!" I exclaimed through my loose teeth and swollen upper lip.

"Where is he?" The detective asked calmly.

Letah and I both looked and each other, remaining quiet. The silence in the room was thick enough to cut with a knife! And then ...

"Don't play with me! This is not a fuckin' game! Your boyfriend is out there with a warrant for his arrest, and an approach with caution advisory over his head. That means if he even so much as sneezes, some nervous ass rookie cop is probably gonna blow his mutha'fuckin head off his shoulders! Is that what you want? Now, tell me where he is!" The detectives voice broke through the dead silence like a brick through a plate glass window! And I fell into small pieces.

"I don't know, I swear! But he'll be back here to see about me, he wont stay away with me here! Please don't hurt him!"

The detective grabbed his cell phone, punching the life out of the buttons! "This is detective Rick Connor at Sharp Memorial, working the Davis assault case. Hey listen, I just got a possible lead on the Iesha Ellis murder case..." I was sick to my stomach as he coldly and matter of factly spoke to who ever was on the other end. He talked about Chance like he was talking about an animal they were hunting!

Unknown to all of us, Chance had gone back to the house to get some clean clothes and, to talk to Linn, to try and explain everything that happened. Still in the car, he sat in the driveway and leaned back in the seat to catch his breath for a moment. The first thing that he wondered was, who could have done this to Iesha, second thing he thought was, how badly he had wanted to hurt her for what she had done to us, and that his intentions were to go over there and fuck her up. Somewhere deep down inside he was glad that he didn't, but he wasn't the least bit sorry for her. After all, if she had been any where near as foul to anybody else as she had been to me, she had it coming. He just hated the fact that he had to be the one to walk smack dab into the middle of the shit, literally!

Chance was so tired, physically, mentally and in every other way you could image from all the shit I had taken him through over the past two months. So he put his head back against the seat and closed his eyes. Just then he heard a click as he opened his eyes to find the end of a nine-millimeter handgun pressed up against the side of his head. It was a deputy from the San Diego County Sheriff's Department. "Evan Chance, you are under arrest for suspicion of murder, put your hands on the steering wheel and don't move!

At the same time Linn was also placed under arrest for Davis's murder. They carefully placed her inside an ambulance and escorted her to the infirmary at the Justice Center, where she gave a full confession. It turns out that she had been slowly poisoning my stepfather with arsenic, because of all the medications he was on, it was difficult to distinguish the difference between possible drug interaction and him actually being poisoned until an autopsy was performed. The detective asked why she did it and here is what she said.

The day that Lady-Bird died, Linn was at home with her. They had been playing hide and go seek when Davis came home for lunch, that's when him and Lady-Bird started to argue, Linn said that she heard her tell Davis that she knew what he had been doing to Letah and she was gonna go to the police. Linn said that Davis told Lady-Bird that he would kill her first and then he put his hands around her neck, strangling her to death. Then he picked her up and took her into my room, placed a rope around her neck and hung her from the wood beam in the ceiling. Linn was behind the door hiding, he never even noticed her.

I'm laying in that hospital bed bruised and battered, then that fuckin' cop was gettin' on my nerves askin' all those damn questions and going out of my mind with worry about Chance and on top of all this, now I was starting to go into withdrawals again. It had been close to 12 hours now since my last fix, so the cramps and fatigue were kicking back in. It felt like I was itching inside and I couldn't keep still! The only thing that was really saving me from going completely nuts was the morphine drip they had me on for the pain. But I still needed a hit. My body craved it! And in a short while I knew I would be crying for it! So, I begged Letah to go out to the car and get the stash that I had bought earlier that night. She didn't want to, but I insisted, so she finally gave in, only after I promised on Lady-Bird's grave that this would be the last time.

While I waited on her to get back, I figured I would turn on the TV to pass time. I clicked the remote control until I landed on channel 8. Then, I just about swallowed my tongue! There was a picture of Chance being broadcast in connection with Iesha's murder. The reporter was saying something about investigators finding Chance's fingerprints at the scene and surveillance video from the hotel at the time of the murder showing him entering and leaving her suite. They also said that this was a particularly gruesome crime and something about the murderer having removed Iesha's heart from her chest. They also said that chance was being held at the San Diego County Detention Center on a one million cash dollar bond. They were also saying some crazy shit about this being the second time he had been charged with murder. They said the first time that the case was thrown out due to a hung jury or something. He supposedly beat some guy to death in 2001, a football player from N.K.U at a college party. I was in a complete state of shock! What they were just saying could not have been true, Chance and I had been together for over three years and he never even so much as raised a hand to me and I'm supposed to believe that he killed somebody six years ago and never mentioned anything about it. Letah stood at the entrance to the door where she had been standing for about the past five minutes. I didn't even notice her, she walked over to me slowly as I began to cry. "If I had only told Chance the truth about my past when we met none of this would be happening. It's all my fault!" I said. "Looks like you both had some skeletons in the closet." Letah said as she reluctantly handed me the small baggy of heroin and nervously stood watch while I quickly snorted the "real" pain medicine. And like magic, the ache left me as I eased back into the bed and prepared to take flight for one last time. You see, I promise Letah that I was gonna tell my doctor that I was hooked on dope, so that I could start some kind of treatment right away. I had too much to live for to go out like this! And then ...

About twenty minutes later I went into heart failure and slip into a comma due to a bad interaction from the mixture of heroin and morphine. The doctors worked on me for the next two hours, but it was no use. I died at 8:47pm. The toxicology report showed high amounts of heroin in my bloodstream, cause of death was rule an overdose, enough to kill a horse they said.

Even with all of his family's money and influence behind him, Chance spent the next two weeks in police custody, the district attorney managed to convince the judge that he was a flight risk and an extreme threat to the community, so his bond was revoked. Shortly after that some new evidence was introduced that proved Chance's innocence and cleared him on all charges, so he was finally released. With his life shattered and his heart broken into a thousand pieces over my death, he returned back to Chicago, placed his house up for sale and disappeared, nobody has seen or heard from him since. My fear and my lies destroyed the only man I ever loved!

Apparently Frank Jordan the Congressman from Chicago that Iesha was gamin', finally got wise and when he figured out that he could never really have her, no matter how much he loved her or how much that he gave her, he had some of his goons track her down and wipe her out. He had fallen deeply in love with her and was determined to have her heart, one way or another, so he had his boys remove it from her body and bring it to him, he said, "that way, he knew he would always have it." One of the men that was paid to kill her suddenly found religion and developed a conscience. Ain't that a bitch! He blew his own brains out, but before he did, he left a note confessing to God and to man every filthy deed he had ever committed. Among them was Iesha's brutal murder. The Cook County district attorney's office immediately issued a search warrant for the Congressman's home, there they found all the evidence they needed to gain an indictment on a capital murder charge, in addition to a felony charge for gross abuse of a corpse. They also arrested the other fools who were responsible for Iesha's death, among them was my ex-boyfriend Tico, it turns out that he had actually met the Congressman through Iesha when he got out of prison, he was hired to handle some of the Congressman's "dirty" street business. Tico also admitted to attacking me at the hotel that same night, he said that it was payback for setting him up, which I did in order to escape him 4 years ago. It also turns out that Tico was actually the one who cut Iesha open and removed her heart (while she was still alive!) He told her that this was payback for all the hearts she had stolen in her life. I always knew that he was a cold-blooded mutha'fucka, but what he did to Iesha was just sick! I guess the "*chance she took*" ended up costing her dearly! Just like mine ultimately cost me everything that I had cherished and waited so long for, my peace, my happiness, my new life and my "Chance".

Preface

As the early autumn rains started to fall, I stood outside on the wood deck, staring at the ocean with tears in my eyes. I watched the waves crash against the sandy shoreline of the beach as the wind began to pick up. It was hurricane season in Miami.

From behind me, I heard the sound of the glass patio door slide open. It was Chance. I heard his footsteps move toward me, but I never turned around. I didn't want him to see that I had been crying again, but he didn't need to see my face, because he always knew when I was hurting. It seemed like he could just feel it!

Chance walked up and stood right behind me. With my back still turned, he put his arms around my waist and held me close. As he softly kissed the back of my neck and shoulders, a heavenly chill went down my spine. He had never touched me that way before! His hands were warm and strong. His kisses were tender and sweet. I was comforted instantly. His touch sent a rush all the way through me that made my whole body hot! I had been waiting for this for so long!

I turned around to face him. Then, with out even so much as a single word, he slowly pressed his soft, full lips against mine. I reached up and slid the tips of my fingers against his smooth baldhead, as the rain washed over us both. His powerful arms tightened down around me like two steel bands that I could not have escaped, even if I had wanted to. Which I didn't, not even in the least!

Slowly I ran my hands underneath his soaking wet tank top as the rain started to pour and he squeezed me even tighter. Our eyes locked, as the wind blew and the storm began around us! I reached out and touched his chest and proceeded to slide my hands all over his hard, muscular frame. His pecks rippled and flexed as he grabbed me around the waist and lifted me up on to the wooden patio guard railing, kissing and biting me on the neck, while I grew hotter and hotter!

Then he wrapped his fist around the collar of my t-shirt and ripped it straight down the middle, exposing both of my breasts. He held them in his hands and licked the droplets of rain from my nipples. I was under his complete control! I put my arms around his neck as he tore my panties apart at the seams and snatched them off of me. He put his arms back around me and kissed me deeply as I reached down into his shorts. I gasped as I touched his manhood. It was so long and so hard! "Hell, who am I kidding?" It was huge! Now we were both ready.

Chance then braced himself firmly against me. Our bodies pressed against one another, my dark brown skin against his dark brown skin. I could feel it as my body screamed his name out loud. He was my fantasy, the fantasy that had played over and over again inside my head for the past year. He was now everything to me! He was all that I had known inside my dreams, and this was going to be my ultimate expression of love. This was to be my first time!

My clitoris thumped out a peculiar beat as I took the tip of his dick between my fingers and wedged it against the juicy entrance of my vagina. I was throbbing! I wanted it, but I was scared! Chance sensed my fear and paused, looking deeply into my eyes through the constant downpour of rain. I kissed his lips and took the deepest breath of my life as he pushed himself inside me.

I then wrapped my legs around him as he picked me up off of the wood railing, slowly stroking me back and forth. I put my arms around his neck as he held me up in the air. I squeezed his massive arms as they flexed. With his hard dick still inside me, he carried me into the house, grunting as he forcefully slid the heavy glass door back open to make his way through the kitchen and over to the white cushioned wicker sofa in the sunroom that faced outward at the beach, where the storm pounded the foamy surf against the shore.

Chance laid me down on the sofa and stepped out of his boxers, with his dick sharply at attention. I could still smell the sweet sea breeze as it blew in through the open door. I could still hear the waves crashing outside almost in perfect time with the sound of my own beating heart, while Joe sang "If I Was Yo' Man" over the Bose Stereo System.

Chance kneeled down before me and kissed me. Then he moved down to my neck, my breast, and my stomach as he kissed my thighs and parted my legs. He softly tongued my pussy, slowly and deeply. I came almost right away! I began to moan out of control as he took his time and tasted every single drop of my love. Every little drip drop!

After what had to be two or three of the most intense orgasms known to man, Chance pulled himself up toward me at eye level and slowly worked his dick back inside me. It was so intense that I could not help but dig my nails into his dark chocolate skin. He dug himself deeper inside me. I shuttered as he tapped what I guess was my "G-Spot"! Over and over and over again! A scream of passion escaped from my lips.

Then, he put my legs up in the air and began to fuck me slowly, taking his time. Pushing his dick all the way inside me and then pulling it all the way out, again and again. I was in the sweetest of agony and the river that flowed from inside me was the proof. I would have never imagined that I could feel so good. My heart began to race out of control and my pussy started to quiver in an unusually intense spasm. I wanted to scream but I couldn't catch my breath!

Chance plunged and thrust himself inside me, until he started to go into his own ecstatic spasm and then he squeezed me and shouted out loud "Oh, Angell! Yes! Yes!" as he released every drop of passion that was inside.

He trembled as I touched his dark brown skin. I could feel the goose bumps raise up on his arms as he lay next to me. Then, Chance put his arms around me, holding me close to his heart and I drifted peacefully off to sleep as he kissed my lips goodnight.

And then came the drama!

CHAPTER 1

Webster's dictionary defines the word "chance" as an accidental happening of events and a calculation of probable or possible risk.

It's incredible how one little word can change your life in so many ways. The great early American writer Walter Inglis Anderson once said that, "our lives can only improve when we take chances, and the first, most difficult risk that we can take is to be honest with ourselves". Truer words have never been spoken!

I grew up as an only child. My father was a born again, bible believing, tongue talkin', apostolic preacher and mother was a devoted wife and homemaker.

We didn't have a lot of material things, but then again my mother always said that as long as we had God and each other, that's all we needed. We had the perfect family.

It was 1990. I was ten years old and we lived in the poorest section of Miami known as Overtown. The neighborhood had just been ripped to pieces by riots the year before and was still aching and torn apart.

It was also just about then that crack cocaine had been introduced and had started to take control of the ghettos. They called it "The Rock", cuz it was hittin' everybody in one-way or another. Because you were either smoking it, selling it, or you knew somebody that was smoking it or selling it. Whether you liked it or not!

Almost overnight "The Rock" had taken the poorest community in America and brought it even further to its knees. It was like a nightmare. I mean picture this, take a large neighborhood full of desperate people who were already struggling just to survive from day to day. Now add 5 times as many murders, 10 times the mayhem, and then sprinkle that with more pimpin', prostitution and panhandlin' than even the most corrupted criminal mind could conceive. That was Overtown in 1990.

I mean, it already had to be one of the saddest, most hopeless places in the world, but now on top of that, it had gotten straight up scary!

That's also where my grandpa's church was. He was a pastor for over thirty-five years. My father took over after he passed away. But before he died, my grandpa made my father promise that he would never let the doors of the church close and that he would always be there to help those in need. He said that God would be the only one who could save the people of Overtown and Liberty City.

So, my father promised that the doors of the church would remain open as long as he was alive. So, we moved from Liberty City, which was about five minutes away, to my Grandpa's house in Overtown, which sat right behind the church.

Because my father was the church pastor, we lived in the house right behind the church. That meant that people were coming to him with their problems, day and night. Sometimes he hardly got any sleep.

We lived in the most crime ridden, drug infested part of the city. So, my father spent a lot of his time counseling crackheads and the people who loved them.

My father would spend most of his time at the church, and even though he was usually only right next-door, he stayed so involved with everybody else's problems, that I really hardly saw him. And when I did, he was in such a rush or in such deep thought that he hardly had the time or energy for my mother and me.

Mama would always say that my father worked for the Lord and the "Lord's business came first. She had learned to accept the calling that was placed on his life. She used to say that she would rather have a man who was busy with God, than a man who was busy with the work of the devil. And God sure did keep him busy.

She didn't really get to spend a whole lotta' time with my father, but she understood. She looked at being his wife as her mission, her ministry, and the job that she was given by God. By loving and supporting my father with his ministry, she was making a sacrifice for the Lord. That is where she found her comfort.

My mother ran a food pantry for the hungry. People from all over the neighborhood use to come and get groceries for the their families. There were mothers with their children that probably would not have made it through the month without help from the pantry.

You would have been surprised at how many people didn't have enough to eat. This is where I learned the importance of giving and lending a helping hand to those in need.

My mother had a heart of gold. She would give her last to anybody. I saw how her kindness touched so many people. She was my hero and I wanted to be just like her.

She was beautiful inside and out. She was a gorgeous woman with a flawless complexion of dark chocolate, with eyes to match, and her hair was jet black and bone straight. And she had the most beautiful high cheekbones that were placed just right. Her nose was keen and perfect. Her teeth were a blinding white that stood evenly in line, one beside the other. People always said that she looked Natalie Cole, only not quite as tall, but still just as gorgeous and curvy.

Everybody would tell me that someday I was gonna grow up to look just like my mother. And I couldn't wait. I was so skinny and awkward and she was so dark and lovely and perfect.

I spent a lot of time helping my mother at the pantry, stocking the shelves, cleaning, dusting, and doing inventory and stuff like that.

Though it was a free food pantry, my mother ran it pretty much like a regular grocery store. She treated everybody that came for food with nothing but dignity and respect. She was always kind and they were always treated like human beings.

My mother would tell me. "Angell, we are all just a circumstance away from being in need. And in the end, when it really comes down to it, we are all in God's hands and everything we have belongs to him."

She believed that no man, woman or child should ever go hungry if we could help them. I never forgot that. She use to say that it was every person's responsibility to do what he could for his brother and that we should never look down on anyone.

My mother would try to help people who were down on their luck with finding jobs and housing. She use to work for the Dade County Board of Education. So, she still had a lot of connections with the county. That's also how she got the city's support and sponsorship money to run the food pantry, along with private donations. But a lot of the money came from state and county grants.

Sometimes it was a real struggle to keep the pantry going. What's crazy is, we were barely making it ourselves, yet a lot of times we were the only hope some of the people in the neighborhood had, especially the old people.

After school in the afternoons, me and my mother would get in our old beat up church van and go deliver meals to sick and shut ins around Overtown and Liberty City. Sometimes it made me cry when I thought about how many people would go hungry if we had not brought them food.

CHAPTER 2

There was a young girl that lived not too far from us, she couldn't have been more than nineteen or twenty years old, with four small children. We would stop by her house from time to time & bring little things for the kids; she had a five year old, a three year old, a one year old and a newborn that was just three months.

Her name was Javette; she lived in a run down project apartment on 15th, in a building that should have been demolished years ago. You could smell the stench of stale piss coming from the side of the building. There were six big plastic garbage cans that always sat at the curb overflowing, with small white maggots crawling along the edges. It made my skin crawl.

"Come on baby, grab this bag and be careful not to drop anything. This is something real special for the kids. Hurry up now; we got three more stops to make before it gets dark. And we still gotta get home in time to make dinner for your father", my mother said as we both hurried along the broken sidewalk, past four well dressed dope boys who stood off to the side of the building making deals wit' dirty fiends that danced anxiously in place waiting to be served "the magic fix".

I was fourteen years old but still very much a little girl. Being raised up in the church kept me from being exposed to a lot of things. I don't know if that was good or bad. At my age, most girls had seen it all, and done more than their share too.

But anyway, as I walked behind my mother, the scent of her perfume almost seemed to cover the foul smell of the projects. Although I was born and raised in the hood, poverty and hopelessness is something that you never really get use to, even though you see it everyday.

The hair on the back of my neck stood up as we walked through the stinking hallway and rang the buzzer. Javette opened the door as the loud pungent odor of shitty diapers, mixed with the smell of stale weed and beer just about caused me to gag.

"Hi Miss Sarah! Come on in! Is all that for us? You ain't have to bring us all this. I told you I was suppose to start back gettin' my food stamps this month. I put Rick's ass out again and went down to the welfare. I'm gon' be getting like $813 in stamps and I got an appointment wit' child support tomorrow. He just started working for the city, making $14 an hour, doin beach clean up and I'm finna' stroke his ass." Javette said as she walked away from the door carrying her one year old on her hip, while tilting her head to the side to hold the telephone against her shoulder, still talking indirectly to whoever was on the other end. Her hair was in complete disarray, standing wildly all over her head, with some of the tracks showing from her sweated out weave.

"Girl, this is the lady from the church. I'ma call you back in a minute. Yeah girl! And call them one niggas we met at the park the other day. Tell 'em it's finna go down! Aight, it's on!" She said as she held a Black n' Mild in the corner of her mouth, while me and my mother brought the packages inside and sat them on the kitchen table. Javette watched as we began to unpack the bags.

"I brought the kids some shoes. School will be starting soon and I figured they could use them. I also brought over a few things you're your brother Jayvin. " My mother said as Javette stood back with a look of slight discontent.

"Oh. Jayvin ain't gon' wear this stuff, it ain't even got no name brand on it! And my kids only wear Jordan's" she said ungratefully. Jayvin was Javette's seventeen-year old brother that lived with her because their mother was so strung out on crack cocaine, that she was unable to care for him anymore.

Javette pushed the shoes back toward my mother and non-chalantly flicked her Black-n-Mild into the dirty ashtray that sat on the kitchen counter next to an open jar of baby food.

Then, from the back room you could hear the sound of two children arguing as one of them began to cry. Javette ran to the back almost in a rage and began to scream out of control at the two children as my mother stood at the table unpacking some more of the things we had brought over.

"You black ass bastard, I'ma beat the shit outta you! Why the fuck you spill this goddamn cereal all over my floor? Get the fuck up and go in the living room before I brake yo' neck! And hurry the fuck up, lookin' like yo' ugly ass daddy!" She shouted as a loud slap from her hand cracked across the tender skin of the oldest child.

"Oww! Mommy, I'm sorry! I ain't gon' do it no more!" The little boy shrieked in agony as he ran into the living room and stood next to the sofa with his head down, tears streaming like a salty river down his ashy little face that had yet to be bathed.

"And shut the fuck up! Before I come in there and give yo' ass somethin' to really cry about!" Javette yelled from the other room.

I was in shock! I had never seen anything like that before. My mother and father never talked to me like that. And I had only gotten one spanking in my whole life and compared to this, what I had gotten wasn't a spanking at all. Listening to Javette slap her son was the equivalent of watching a really gruesome horror movie or slasher film. It scared me to death.

"Did you hear what the fuck I just said? Shut 'cho goddamn mouth! Shut up I said!" Javette shouted as she raced from the back room and ran toward the child with her hand raised again to strike him. But before she could, my mother dashed across the room and threw herself in between Javette's open palm and her son.

"You hold it right there! I dun' set here and listened to just about enough! Don't 'chu put 'cho hands on this boy again! I mean it! You must be outta yo' mind, beatin' on these kids like that! You could hurt one of them, or worse! You better get a hold of yo' self or I will have children's protective services up and through here so fast, you wont know what hit 'chu! Or maybe that's what 'chu need!" My mother said as she put her hands on her hips and looked Javette straight in the eye without flinching.

"Miss Sarah, you don't understand! These kids be gettin' on my nerves! I just can't take it! And now, ain't neither one of their no good daddies nowhere to be found! I'm tired Miss Sarah! I can't do this by myself!! I need some help! Please! Miss Sarah I need some help before I go crazy!" Javette said as she slid to the floor on her knees next to her son and put her arms around him and began to sob.

"Mommy sorry! Mommy sorry! Mommy is so sorry!" Javette sobbed through her own river of tears.

"It's gon' be alright child. I'm prayin' for you. The Lord gon' see you through. And I'm gon' help you too. It's okay. It's okay." My mother said as she sat down on the filthy carpet next to Javette and held her, wiping her tears as she cried long and hard.

Me and my mother were just about ready to leave. Javette wiped her face again and stood to her feet with her little boy in her arms. She thanked my mother for coming by and for all the gifts.

Just then the baby began to fuss from the other side of the room in her crib. So, Javette put the oldest child down and hurried over to the baby immediately picking her up and putting a sour milk bottle into her mouth to quiet her.

My mother looked over at Javette and shook her head.

"Children are a blessing from God. Don't ever forget that." My mother said as she placed her hands on the door. But before she could turn the knob there was a loud knocking from the other side.

"BAM! BAM! BAM! BAM! BAM! BAM!"

Went the beating at the door.

"Girl, open the door! It's me!" An impatient male voice shouted from the other side.

Javette put the baby back down in her crib and quickly hustled to the door. She looked out of the peephole and hurriedly opened the latch.

"Bitch, you heard me knockin'! Move! Damn! Where my food at? Better have my shit ready! Cuz, I'm hungry than a mutha'fucka!" It was a short boney light skinned nigga wearing a crispy snow white Polo jogging suit and a brand new pair of Air Jordan's.

He was one of the little dope boys we passed outside when we were on our way in the building. He rushed in as Javette opened the door and looked at my mother and me in surprise.

"Miss Sarah, this is my new boyfriend, Kevin. Umm… Kevin, this is Ms. Sarah from the church", Javette said uncomfortably, holding her head down as if she was ashamed.

"Oh, yeah. What's up, Ms Sarah? How you doin'", the thuggish young dope boy said, rushing by Javette, handing her fat wad of cash as his beeper sounded, sending him racing over to the phone. He dialed anxiously.

"Hey, what up Bigman? Naw, I'm 'bouta bag this shit up and head back out to the trap. (Kevin paused and listened) Hey, hold on dog! Ain't nobody playin' wit' cho money! I told you. I got 'cho shit! I'm over my girl house on 15th …", the young thug said to who ever was on the other end of the phone.

Javette stood perfectly still without saying a word, the cash held tightly in her grasp. But her eyes remained trained on the floor; so as to avoid making contact with my mother's stare of disapproval.

"Wait a minute! Weren't you just balled up on the floor cryin' about havin' all these kids and their daddies not being around to help. So, now you got this new boy runnin' in and out of here wit' dope and layin' up in front of yo' kids. And don't 'chu look at me like I'm crazy! I know I just saw him outside slaggin' rocks wit' three other knuckleheads. Why do you keep taking these kinds of risks wit' cho life? Didn't you just hear the conversation he was having on the phone? Somebody could come in here tonight and kill him, you and yo' babies! Then what?" My mother paused and shook her head.

"Now, I know you need help, but trust me when I say that this ain't the kinda' help you need. You have got to start thinkin' and makin' better decisions! Because the choices you make today, will be the consequences you may have to live with for years to come", my mother said to Javette as she touched her cheek that was still wet with tears.

"I'll be back by here tomorrow morning at about 11:30 or so. We gon' start gettin' you together." My mother added as we walked out of the door. Javette remained in the doorway frozen as though she was suspended in animation, with her hand still clutching the dirty dope money. My mother and I walked out into the filthy hallway that smelled like piss. I held my breath until we made it outside. But there was no escape from the foul stench of poverty and ignorance that constantly surrounded those who found themselves imprisoned in the hood.

"That's why I always tell you to be a good girl! Study hard! Get 'chu a good education and don't be messin' wit' these little hard head boys out here in these streets, because that could be you in a few years if you don't keep walkin' wit the Lord! That girl coulda' been something, but her momma and daddy started messin' around wit' that dope and just lost their minds. And before anybody knew it, the girl was fourteen years old and pregnant, just a child herself and about to be a mother..."

My mother said as we made our way back to the van to finish the rest of our stops. Her voice seemed to almost fade away as I looked back at Javette. Ours eyes connected, and for just that brief moment I could feel the pain of where she had been and the things she had seen and been through.

Her eyes penetrated me as I stood by the van in the choking Miami ghetto heat. I felt her envy, longing to go back in time so that she could be fourteen again and undo all the mistakes she had made. But sometimes there's no turning back and all the praying in the world won't convince time to slow up.

Later that night my mother received a phone call. I knew that something had gone terribly wrong by the way she screamed and called on God, saying, "Jesus, help us!" instantly flipping into automatic prayer mode.

It was my mother's best friend Sister Walls, she was my mother's prayer partner, she was calling to tell us that, about an hour earlier three niggas wearing ski masks and dressed in all black kicked down Javette's door, came in and shot everybody in the house, even the babies. Sister Walls didn't know it but Bigman gave the order that nobody was to be left alive. There were no survivors except for her little brother Jayvin who just so happened to be out at a football game with some friends. He returned to find the only family that he had, slaughtered!

Apparently Javette's new boyfriend was hustlin' for Bigman, one of Miami's most notorious and dangerous dopemen. Bigman had the hood on lock, and in Liberty City, nobody even so much as sneezed without getting his permission, not even the police.

The word on the street was that Kevin had been skimming money off the top for about a year. It was never anything much, never anything too noticeable, just a fifty here or a hundred there. But Bigman counted every dollar, so it wasn't too long before he got wise to Kevin. And when he did, he had to make an example out of him for everybody in Liberty City to see.

The first thing you learn about the dope game is to never bite the hand that feeds you. You don't ever jerk the nigga you work for! I guess Kevin should have studied his hustla's handbook a little bit harder.

And as for Javette, she was taking way too many chances with her life. Where I was from it was typical for the young girls with babies to move some little dope-boy into her crib that she barely knew. It didn't even have to be her baby's daddy either. The only real qualification that a nigga had to have was a car with some shiny rims, a fresh pair of the latest gym shoes, and a few dollars to buy weed and pay her rent. Which usually didn't amount to much more than twenty five or thirty dollars a month because she had Section-8 housing. This was the standard for young girls like Javette that lived in the projects.

But then again, maybe she really didn't have all that many choices. Her parents were both drug addicts; she was basically left to raise herself and her brother. She became a teenage mother over and over and over again. She got involved with one guy after another that really didn't care anything about her or her kids. But as long as a guy looked like he had what she wanted on the surface she didn't care how it ended up.

When I found out about what happened to Javette and her kids it broke my heart. I spent the next few weeks with her heavy on my mind. I would go from trying to put it out of my head all together, to trying to figure out how her life could have gone so terribly wrong. I was left with so many questions.

Maybe nobody loved her enough. Maybe she just didn't love herself. Maybe she just didn't love her children. Maybe she didn't even know how to love at all. Maybe nobody other than my mother ever told her that God loved her and that she deserved all the best that life had to offer. And maybe by the time my mother reached Javette it was already to late. Maybe her destiny had already been sealed.

All the obstacles that stood in front of her probably clouded Javette's view of the world. Sometimes it's hard to see the forest because of the trees that block our vision. The old black folks use to say that if we knew better, we would do better. Maybe that's true and maybe it' ain't, but I knew one thing for sure, I had already decided that I was never going to do the things she did. I had made my mind up that I was never going to end up like Javette. I would never open my legs to just any old Tom, Dick, and Harry that came along trying to tell me what they thought I might be dumb enough to fall for. I was never gonna let some little thugged out gym shoe hustla' get me knock me up and leave me stuck high and dry with a crying baby or an STD that I could never get rid of.

I was never to take the kinds of risks or chances that destroyed Javette's life and the lives of so many girls like her that came from the projects.

.

CHAPTER 3

That same summer that Javette was murdered, an old lady by the name of Mrs. Trenton moved into the house next door to us. Her brother Elder Trenton (who sat on the trustee board of our church) had died and left her the property. She had a granddaughter named Pleasure who lived with her and was just about my age.

Anyway, seeing as how they were new to the neighborhood, my mother thought it would be a nice gesture to bake a cake and take it over as sort of a welcome gift.

So me and my mother went over to the house and knocked on the screen door.

KNOCK KNOCK KNOCK

There was no answer.

"Maybe they ain't home, momma. Let's go." I said impatiently, with my wishful eyes set on that delicious double chocolate cake, hoping we'd get to take it back home and slice in to it. I could almost taste the rich chocolate through the plastic Tupperware dish.

KNOCK KNOCK KNOCK KNOCK

And there was still no answer.

"Hello, it's Sarah Epps from next door. Is anybody home?" My mother yelled through the raggedy screen door as we swatted at two giant horse flies that circled around us also hoping for a share of the delicious treat.

Then sound of approaching footsteps came from inside the house. And the voice of an old woman screeched aloud like an eagle.

"Who is it? Who is that bammin' on my door? I dun' told y'all, I ain't got no kool-aid, no sugar, no milk, no butter, no eggs, no syrup, no cigarettes and nothing else! So you can just get 'cho ass off my porch! Go on! Get! I meant it!"

The old woman yelled as she got closer to the door.

"Hi, Sister Trenton! It's Sarah Epps from next door. I just came by to say hi and bring you and your granddaughter a cake I made. My husband is the pastor of the church your brother use to attend", my mother quickly said to the angry old woman before she had a chance to go off again.

"Oh, yeah! The same church that's trying to get me to sell them this property, huh?" (Mrs. Trenton shook her head and leaned against the frame of the door as she was exhausted) "I met the pastor yesterday. I'm sorry! I didn't mean no harm. You just wouldn't believe it, I ain't been moved in here more than a few weeks and these crazy folks around here already comin' over here knockin and beggin' and carryin' on! And them little thugs on that corner keep tryin' to get at my lil' grandbaby. I dun' had to call the police 4 times in the past three days" Mrs. Trenton said as she mean mugged the young hustlas that stood across the street openly slangin' "da' rock".

"I know exactly what 'chu mean! I run the food pantry next door, so you can just imagine what I go through everyday. All we can do is pray for 'em" my mother responded.

"I'm gon' do more than pray! I'm gon' keep on callin' the police 'til they realize that them and nobody else ain't finna run me away from here. And I ain't sellin' my place to the church either! This was my brother's house and when he died he left it to me, and I ain't goin' no place.

And then again, I don't know. Maybe I should just sell it. The fire marshal came by last week to inspect, and said that I had a lot of faulty wiring in here. I don't know what I'm gonna do. Y'all come on in if ya' comin'. Ya' lettin' flies in!" Mrs. Trenton said as she held the screen door open, inviting us in.

Mrs. Trenton was a very petite old light skinned woman with long silver hair that had been neatly pulled back into a ponytail. Her grey eyes had grown old and tired and the wrinkles on her skin confessed the many struggles of her seventy plus years.

"Oh, thank you, this is a beautiful cake! Hold on a minute. Lemme call my granddaughter, so y'all can meet her too. (Mrs. Trenton turned to the screen door and yelled) "Pleasure! Come in here! We got guests!" Mrs. Trenton stood at the screen door and watched her grand daughter that was outside by the house, talking to one of the corner hustlas that was leaning up against his flashy car trying to impress her as he spit his game. Mrs. Trenton took a deep breath and sighed. "I swear, this child is gonna be the death of me! I just know it! I gotta constantly watch her, cuz' she's hot and fast" she added tiredly.

"Mam!" Her granddaughter answered as she came stomping through the door, standing with her arms folded and her glossed up lips twisted to one side.

"This is my grandbaby. Her name is Pleasure. Pleasure, unpoke yo' lips and meet Ms. Sarah and her daughter. Uh... I'm sorry baby. What's yo' name again?" Mrs. Trenton said as she looked at me over the top part of her thick bifocal lenses that were held around her neck by a tarnished metal chain.

"Her name is Angellina, but we call her Angell. Angell say hello to Pleasure.

Pleasure was tall, curvaceous, and extremely well developed for a girl her age. She kind of reminded you of Beyonce. Her complexion was a high yellow that had been softly bronzed by the Miami sunshine and her eyes were a brilliant green that shimmered like the wild grass of the Florida Everglades. Her hair was a thick, dirty red that hung down past her shoulders in a bone straight perm. Her posture was strong and defiant. And though she had just entered her teens, Pleasure had the body of a grown woman, with an attitude to match.

"Y'all go on in the kitchen and cut some of that cake! I got some ice cream in the deep freeze too. It's okay, ain't it Miss Sarah?" Mrs. Trenton asked my mother.

"Of course it is." My mother responded.

"Y'all wash ya' hands. And Pleasure, be sure to clean up ya' mess" old Mrs. Trenton said as me and Pleasure both went off to the kitchen.

"My grandma be trippin'. I can't stand her" Pleasure pouted underneath her as we entered the kitchen outside ear range of her grandmother.

"So, where you from?" I asked Pleasure, trying to break the ice as I sat down at the round wobbly wooden table, while she reached up into the cabinet for two plastic ice cream bowls.

"We from St. Louis. It sho' is hot down here! I feel like I'm 'bouta burn up. You like chocolate or vanilla?", she asked me, opening the deep freezer, pulling out two boxes, as she responded to my question.

"I like chocolate." I said, pointing at the frosted box of ice cream in her right hand.

"Me too. Chocolate is my favorite! Well, right after strawberry. But, we ain't got no strawberry. So, today my favorite is chocolate" Pleasure said as she got two spoons out of the kitchen counter drawer next to the refrigerator.

"So, what are y'all doin' here in Miami?" I asked.

"Well, my momma started smokin' crack, and she couldn't take care of me no more. My great uncle passed away, so we came here to live in his house. My granny thought we needed a change", she said.

"Oh, what about 'cho daddy?" I asked.

"He got shot, hustlin'. My granny always says he's in heaven, but I don't think hustlas go to heaven. Do you?" Pleasure commented as she poked at her cake and ice cream with the plastic spoon.

"I don't know. I don't really know any hustlas. I mean, it's plenty of 'em around here but I don't know 'em. And I don't know where they go when they die. But I could ask my father. He's a preacher. He knows all about the bible and heaven and stuff like that", I responded as Pleasure shed a silent tear that dropped on to the kitchen table.

"It's okay to be sad. My grandpa died and I still miss him. Sometimes I still cry too", I said as we both let a few quiet moments pass before we spoke again.

"So, I guess you're gonna be going to the junior high school around the corner? That's where I'm going. This will be my first year going to school. I can't wait!" I said, excitedly breaking the somber mood.

"Your first year going to school? You ain't never been to school? So, does that mean you can't read or write?" Pleasure asked as she put her spoon down and looked at me peculiarly.

"Naw girl! I'm home schooled. At least I was until this year. My mother is a teacher. And my father thinks the public schools are too off da' hook! So, my mother gives me my lessons at home. But my mother convinced him that I was old enough to go to the neighborhood school. And girl, I can't wait", I explained.

"That's cool. So, are there any cute boys at this school", Pleasure asked, picking up her spoon and letting melted ice cream drop from it on to her chocolate cake.

"I don't know, I guess. I'm only fourteen and my mother says that I'm too young for boys. I don't need to think about boys 'til I graduate from college and become a teacher like my momma. So who was that boy you were outside talkin' to?" I replied, staring into my bowl of ice cream as if it was a crystal ball and I was seeing the future.

"I don't know, just some nigga from the block, I guess he likes me", Pleasure said casually.

"So, anyway. You gotta a boyfriend?" I asked bashfully.

"Yep!!! Back in St. Louis. His name is Robert, and he looks just like Ralph Tresvant from New Edition, and we kissed on the lips behind his grandmother's garage, and when we get grown, we gon' get married and have two kids, a girl for me and a boy for him. And we gon' name 'em Robbie and Ashley." She rattled off in one whole breath. And my eyes just about popped out of my head with utter surprise. I put my hand over my own mouth to keep myself from laughing too loud.

"Oh my goodness! Girl, you are a trip! You kissed a boy on the lips? I don't believe it! You are lyin'!" I whispered, still giggling with embarrassment.

"Don't tell me you ain't never kissed a boy before. I can't believe you ain't got no boyfriend either. It must not be no cute guys around here." Pleasure said shaking her head.

"I can't have no boyfriend! I told you! I'm just fourteen! My momma and daddy would beat my butt! And besides, I don't even like boys right now" I said, as I looked over at the counter top at all the pots and pans.

"Girl, you trippin'! We gotta find us some boys to kick it wit! I'm gon' hook you up! Maybe if you weren't wearin' those little girl clothes, you could get a boyfriend. What is that you have on anyway, Osh-Kosh? Winnie The Pooh? (Pleasure laughed) And why is yo' hair in that little girl style? Well, never mind, don't worry, I got 'cho back. We gon' get 'chu fixed right up!" Pleasure said as she looked me up and down, rolled her eyes and shook her head again.

"Little girl clothes? Osh-Kosh? Look at 'chu! Walkin' around wit' them little bitty coochie cutter shorts on. You know what? On second thought, I'm gon' hook you up! You gon' have to tone that down around here! Before you be walkin' down the street and get snatched or somethin." I said, as I looked her up and down, rolling my eyes right back at her. And we both busted out laughin' as my mother and her grandma came in to the kitchen.

"What's goin' on in here? Y'all havin some kinda' sugar fit? Well, Sarah. Looks like these two sho' did hit it off." Pleasure's grandma said as she drug herself inside the kitchen and stood with her hands on her hips.

"Come on Angell, it's gettin' late and we gotta get ready for church in the morning" my mother said as she stood behind Pleasure's tiny grandma.

"Momma! Momma guess what? Pleasure is gonna be goin' to the junior high school with me. I'm gon' introduce her to some of the neighborhood kids. Can she come to church with us tomorrow? Please Ma?" I asked my mother anxiously as Pleasure turned and quickly looked at me like I had just lost my mind.

"Well, you know I don't have a problem with it. But that's up to Pleasure's grandmother" My mother said. Mrs. Trenton was standing there in a flower pattern housecoat with an old multicolored apron tied around her waist.

"Fine wit' me. I might even try to make it myself, seeing as how it's just right next door. I mean that's if my arthritis ain't actin' up too bad. This sho' is some strange weather y'all got down here. Seems like it's been rainin' everyday for the past week" her grandma responded as she sat down in one of the rickety wood kitchen chairs to rest her aching legs.

"Would you like to go to Sunday school with Angell?" My mother asked Pleasure.

"I don't like church." Pleasure said quickly.

"Too bad! You're goin' anyway! It ain't gon' hurt 'chu to learn something about The Lord. It'll give you something to do other than listen to that silly rap music" Mrs. Trenton responded. "She's going" her grandma added, looking at Pleasure as if she dared her to talk back.

"Okay. Then I guess it's settled. Pleasure, you be ready at nine o'clock. You can wear pretty much whatever you want. I'll send Angell over here to get 'chu or you can come on over to the house, it sits right behind the church.

Mrs. Trenton, I hope we get to see you tomorrow as well. And it sure was nice to finally meet you!" My mother said, hugging Pleasure and her grandma as we headed out of the door.

"See y'all tomorrow." Pleasure said as she looked over at my mother with the most wide and innocent eyes, the eye that stood in complete contradiction to everything else about her.

CHAPTER 4

Over the next few weeks Pleasure and I hung out almost everyday and on Sundays she would come to church with us. I introduced her to some of the neighborhood kids that I knew, but they didn't really seem to take to Pleasure that well. She was kind of raw and rough around the edges. She had this way of just saying whatever was on her mind, no matter whose feelings it hurt. It was actually sort of funny sometimes.

Like the Saturday afternoon that big booty Dilonda Lovetts came down the street while me and Pleasure were talking to little Vartan Daniels, the silly little boy who carried a football with him everywhere, and seemed to always be around. He was sort of annoying but he was also sort of cute too, so I really didn't mind too much.

Dilonda decided that she was going to walk right over and step in front of us, grab Vartan by the hand and whisper something in his ear. And she wasn't even whispering. Because we heard every word she said.

Dilonda asked Vartan if he liked Pleasure. But before he could even get anything out of his mouth, Pleasure shouted out loud, "Naw he don't like me! Can't you see that he has a crush on Angell?" and then she told Dilonda to take her nappy headed, buck tooth self back up the street and mind her own business, before she went and got a hot comb to straighten out the bee bees on the back of Dilonda's neck. It was so funny! Dilonda went back up the street crying and told her mama that Pleasure threatened to beat her with a hot comb, then her mama came wobblin' her big butt down the street talkin' about, "Did one of y'all say that you were gonna hit my daughter with a straightening comb?"

Pleasure said, "No, but somebody outta'! And they need to get 'chu too while they're at it, cuz both of y'all heads are nappier than the hair on a sheep's ass!"

Me and Vartan were rollin'! Vartan laughed so hard that he dropped his football. So you know it had to be funny. Dilonda and her mother went and told Pleasure's grandma, and Pleasure got her butt beat with a leather belt!

Then we all had to go in the house.

The next day, there was a knock on the screen door. My father was at the kitchen table having breakfast and going over his notes for the morning service. He got up to see who it was.

"Hi, is Angell ready for Sunday school?" Pleasure said as she smacked her lips and popped her bubble gum. She was wearing a black sweater dress that fit her like a second layer of skin, hugging every curve and stopping just at the thigh. It was a really cute little dress (for a hooker).

"Yeah, hold on just a minute, Pleasure. I'll get her for you." My father said as he looked at Pleasure over the top of his glasses and shook his head. Then he called me downstairs to answer the door, grabbed his briefcase and quickly headed over to the church.

"Girl, what is that 'chu got on? We are goin' to church, not to a house party!" I said. I was rather shocked at her inappropriate choice in attire but I don't know why, because she was always trying to wear something that she didn't have any business wearing. Don't get me wrong, I wasn't jealous, or maybe I was just a little bit. But I just couldn't believe her grandma would let her outside wearing some of the stuff she did. The dress showed every twist and turn of her shape, and she knew it. She even had me wishing for a body like hers. But all the wishing in the world wasn't going to help me fill out like that.

"Let's go, before my mama comes in here and gets a good look at 'chu and that dress!" I said hurrying Pleasure out of the back just as I heard my mother's heels against the hardwood stairs.

"You girls ready for Sunday school? I figured we could all walk over together." My mother said as she made her way down the stairs while reading her lesson plan.

"We gon' walk down to the candy store and get some peppermints real quick. We will be back in a minute, mama." I said as I quickly pushed Pleasure out of the door and on to the porch, shutting the door behind us.

"Girl, let's go! Hurry up! We'll go down to the corner and get some candy, and by the time my mother gets her stuff together we'll already be at the church, sittin' down. And maybe she won't notice that tight, too little dress you got on." I said, looking back to make sure that my mother wasn't watching us from the kitchen window as Pleasure and I moved quickly across the grass between the house and the church.

"Dag! Girl, hold up! Lemme holla at my boy!" Pleasure said as she stopped right in her tracks, and gazed across the street at the boys standing in front of a jet black, big body Mercedes Benz s500. Inside the Benz was Bigman's little brother. His name was Lebrian, but they called him Boom-Boom, because he loved to play with firecrackers and blow stuff up. And when you saw him it was never a good sign. Boom-Boom was like the grim reaper, when he was around, somebody usually ended up dead.

But he was cute as hell and he was also one of Miami's most wanted, the police called him a person of interest in more than eleven murders over the last three years. He ran with "The Knock Off Boyz". They were Bigman's death squad. If Bigman wanted somebody dead, these little bad-ass niggas did the job without any remorse. They were also the ones who pulled the hit on Javette and her boyfriend. Those ruthless ass niggas even killed the babies! Now that was worse than heartless.

Boom-Boom sat across the street in his brand new luxury car that had to have cost every bit of $70,000. The bass was bumpin' as he stepped out and handed a bag of dope to one of his boys. Then he looked over at us.

Across the street, me and Pleasure stopped as we were on our way to the corner store. At least that's where we were supposed to be going. But Pleasure had something else in mind as she batted her eyes, licked her lips and stared back across the street at Boom-Boom trying to get his attention. And he took the bait.

"Hey, shawty! Shawty! Come here for a minute!" He said as he nudged his boy that stood to the left of him.

"Who you talkin' to? Me or her?" Pleasure asked, knowing full well who he was talking to.

"You know who I'm talkin' to! I'm talkin' to you, shawty! Come over here and holla at me for a minute. I ain't gon' bite 'chu, unless you want me to. And hurry up before yo' mean ass grandma comes out!" He said as him and his boys laughed out loud and gave each other dap.

"What 'chu doin'?" I asked Pleasure as she started across the street.

"Girl, I'm finna go over here to see what's up wit' dude. He is too cute! He has been tryin' to holla since I moved down here. I heard he gotz mass cheese. Do you see that whip he's pushin'? That's the new Benz! Maybe he'll take us for a ride! Come on!" She said as she switched her over to his car, with her arms swinging at her sides. But I stayed right where I was, as if my feet were cemented into the ground, because I knew better.

"What's up, ma? What 'chu been up to?" Boom-Boom said as he reached out and touched Pleasure's hand.

"Tryin to get wit 'chu." She answered as she flirtatiously licked her lips again, provoking Boom-Boom's advances.

"Girl, that's what's up! But 'cho grandma be buggin'!" Boom-Boom said as he leaned into her and grinned a devilish grin, running his fingers along her arm.

"I'm old enough to talk to who ever I wanna talk to. My grandma don't run me! So what's up?..." Just then, Pleasure was abruptly interrupted by a loud, sharp voice that barked from across the street.

"Pleasure! ... Pleasure Michelle Trenton! What are you doin'? And who is that boy you're talkin' to? Get 'cho fast tail back across this street, right now! And I mean it!" It was her grandma calling to her from the front porch of their house. Pleasure was busted! She turned around startled like a crook caught in the act.

"Oh, snap! It's my granny! I gotta go! I'm gon' page you later!" Pleasure said as she turned and hurried back across the street, passed me and up on to her grandmother's porch.

"What the devil are you doin' over there talkin to those no good thugs. Don't 'chu know that they ain't about nothin' but trouble? You was supposed to be at Sunday school, wit' cho fast tail! Get over to that church! Before I beat the skin off of ya' and turn yo' high yellow ass black and blue! And hurry up!" Pleasure's grandmother yelled as Pleasure pouted and stomped over to the church.

"And y'all get away from over here wit' all that noise! Don't none of y'all live around here! I'm finna call the police! And I'm gon keep callin' em too! You no good vipers! I'm gon' fix it so y'all ain't gon' never be comfortable around here no mo'! Why don't you go somewhere else and sell that smack or crack or whatever is it! You need to be in church! You devils! And stay the hell away from my grand child!" Old Mrs. Trenton shouted across the street at the young gangsters as she drug herself back inside to call the police again, for the 19th time in four days.

"So, that's the old bitch that keeps on callin' five-0, huh? Too bad! Her grand daughter is real, real fly! Too bad! Let's roll niggas!" Boom-Boom said as he chuckled and shook his head, still looking at Mrs. Trenton's run down old house. He hopped back inside his Benz, turned up his beats and got ready to peel away.

"Hey, what's up wit 'chu, lil mama? You wanna ride? Naw, never mind. Girl, you too skinny! Holla at me next year, after you thicken up!" Boom-Boom yelled as him and his boys laughed at me and yelled "Bye-bye blackie!", and laughed out of control, making reference to the darkness of my skin.

My feelings were so hurt. I turned around slowly and started to walk back toward the church to find Pleasure. I knew that those niggas were stupid and would probably never amount to anything, and that I was way too good for either one of them, but it still hurt.

When I got inside the church, Pleasure was sitting at the piano crying. And then before I could say anything, came the most beautiful sound that I had ever heard. Pleasure began to sing. And then she started playing the piano.

"Amazing grace! How sweet the sound, that saved a retch, like me! I once was lost but now I'm found, was blind, but now, I see!" Pleasure sang with the voice of a living angel and touched those piano keys as if she had been taught to play by Beethoven himself.

I was stunned by what I heard. And then my mother walked in behind me and also just stood quietly. We were both in shock. Just looking at this girl dressed in the way too tight black sweater dress, you would have never thought that she could sing like that. That's how ghetto she was. But by the end of the song you could have knocked us both over with a feather. Everybody from Sunday school class was standing at the back of the church with their eyes bucked and mouths wide open.

"Praise the Lord, child! Where did you learn to sing and play the piano like that? You have a wonderful voice!" My mother said as we all gathered around Pleasure.

"My mother taught me. She played the piano at church before she started smokin' crack. I learned from sitting next to her and listening." She said, with teary eyes.

"It's okay child, you don't have to cry no more. Just keep praying for your mother, Jesus gon' make it all right!" (My mother hugged Pleasure) "We are having a music program tonight over at New St. John's. Will you go with us and sing that song? Please!" My mother asked.

"We would love to have you! I heard you singin' too and I was very impressed. The folks over New St. John's would love you!" My father said as he came from behind the baptismal pool, looking like Denzel Washington, twenty years later.

"Well, I don't know. I gotta get ready for the first day of school tomorrow. Plus, my granny needs me to..." Pleasure said as she struggled for an excuse.

"Oh, girl! Come on. We know school starts tomorrow. You will be fine! And I can introduce you to a few girls I know that will be there tonight, some of them go to our school." I said trying to convince her to go, so I wouldn't have to sit by myself.

"Well, okay. I'll go. I'll sing if you want me to." Pleasure said reluctantly.

"Then it's settled! I'll talk to your grandmother and make sure it's okay. But I'm sure she won't mind", my mother said, smiling at Pleasure.

So, we had Sunday school and then morning service. Me and Pleasure sat in the back of the church with most of the other teenagers. At about the end of service, right before the doxology, my father introduced Pleasure as a new neighbor of the church and welcomed her to come back and worship with us again. He also announced that she would be going with us this afternoon at the musical program. You should have heard the church chattering with various comments, some good, and some not so good. But most everybody had something to say, especially "big butt" Dilonda Lovetts.

I couldn't stand her bucktooth, bubble butt ass! She was such a lil ho'. Always flirting and flouncing around in front of all the boys, trying to get attention, especially Vartan. And worst of all, she was always trying to sing. And the bitch couldn't sing her way out of a wet paperbag. Plus, she was always calling me skinny or blackee, or Hershey, it was always something about me being black or skinny. And she always made fun of the nickname my daddy called me, which was "Beanpole". She knew how much I hated it. So she made it point to say it everytime she saw me, and because of that I was so glad to see how upset she got watching Pleasure steal the spotlight.

When everybody was coming up to Pleasure to say hello and welcome her, Dilonda just sat back with her arms folded and rolled her eyes. I guess she didn't like the fact somebody other than her was about to start getting some attention for singing. But at least Pleasure could sing, which was more than I could say for Dilonda.

And she really hated the way all boys looked at Pleasure and how they tried to find a way to be around her. Dilonda was the church ho' and she didn't like the idea of having any competition. But now she had Pleasure to deal with.

CHAPTER 5

After church, everybody went home to eat and relax and get ready for the afternoon musical program across town. Pleasure and some of the other folks from church came back to our house to have supper. My mother always cooked a big dinner on Sundays, because some of the deacons and other people would always come by. Her best friend, Sister Walls usually helped and ate with us too, because she was a widow that lived alone. Her and my mother were also prayer partners.

Me and Pleasure helped my mother and Sister Walls get dinner ready. My father, Deacon Vaughn, Deacon Lestur, Elder Culston and Bishop Linx all sat out in the living room and waited for the food to be served.

Deacon Vaughn said "So, whose child is that in there with Angell? I heard she has a beautiful voice."

"Well, that's Elder Trenton's grandniece, her and her grandmother just moved into the house next door", my father replied leaning back in his easy chair.

,

"Ain't that the house he left to the church? I thought we were supposed to get that property and sell it to the city? He assured us that when he died, the property would come straight to the church board and we would do what we had to do with it." Bishop Linx said as he sat his glass of ice water down and lowered his voice to a sneaky whisper.

"Yeah, I know. But after his death, his sister popped up to claim the house. She said that they hadn't spoken in years, but she was his next of kin. So...", my daddy said in lower tone as he sipped his lemon-aid.

"So? So what? We stood to make alotta money on this deal with the city. And the deal was for both pieces of property, this one here and Elder Trenton's place. We already own the other surrounding buildings on the block. All we needed was that one next door! Will she sell?" Elder Culston whispered.

"I don't know. But now ain't the time to discuss this..." (My father paused) "Hey Bean Pole! How's that food comin'? Sho' do smell good! Tell ya' mama to hurry up! She got five hungry men out here." My father said as Pleasure and I walked into the room unintentionally startling him.

"Mama sent us in here to let y'all know that it's almost ready, and for everyone to go wash their hands." I said as I looked around sensing their immediate discomfort. Pleasure and I slowly walked back to the kitchen with all their eyes upon us.

"Mmm... So, that's Elder Trenton's grand niece, huh? Sho' is pretty, she's a healthy lookin' young thang! I mean... she's very... tall for her age. Mmm, mmm, mmm!" Elder Culston said as he reached inside his suit coat for a napkin to wipe the sweat from his forehead caused by his obvious excitement over Pleasure.

Elder Culston was an old freak that liked young girls. About ten years before, he had been accused of being involved in a sexual relationship with a fourteen-year old run away from Tampa. The story was that she had been staying in an apartment that he owned and that she was basically his under aged mistress. The relationship lasted about six months, until he was eventually found out and arrested.

Once the news reached his wife and the media, he then came to the church seeking counseling and forgiveness from the Lord. But he was obviously still struggling with the same issues, just judging by the way he sat there sweating and salivating over Pleasure's prematurely curvaceous figure. My father, along with the other men in the room just looked at him curiously.

"Anyway, there's too much money on the table to let some long lost sister that we never even heard of stand in the way of this deal! I say after we eat, we all go over and have a little talk with her." Deacon Lestur said anxiously.

"I told you to lemme handle this! I think I can get her to see things our way. I just need y'all to trust me, and lemme handle it. Now, enough of this! I don't know about y'all but I am starvin'! Let's go eat." My father said as he stood up and motioned to the men.

As we all sat down in the dining room to eat, the tension between the men was as heavy as my mother's fresh buttermilk cornbread. We passed each dish around the table and the silence thickened.

Then after one of the most amazing Sunday dinners in history, everybody loaded up in the church van and headed over to New St. John's for the twenty-first annual gospel music celebration. It was a musical event held at the end of each summer to celebrate the history of the black Pentecostal church in Miami.

It was a real big event. Churches from all over Florida came to participate. It was like a who's who of the southern black Christian community. My grandfather use to sit on the board of elders, my father was nominated to take his place. My granddad would have been so proud.

As we approached the church across town, you could feel the music coming from down the street, there were cars and buses lined up for blocks. But we pulled right into the back of the church. There was a spot reserved just for us.

The church was huge! It was a brand new beautiful $3,000,000 state of the art complex with gold trim through out, it was like a palace. But right across the street stood all the neighborhood hustlas and dope boys. And on the next corner stood the dope feinds and geekers. And on the opposite corner was the neighborhood liquor store where everybody came together as one. Even at that young age, the contrast boggled my mind!

When we walked into the main sanctuary, The Tampa Bay Church of Deliverance and

Repentance was singing "Near The Cross". The atmosphere was electric. I mean, church folks always talk about feeling the spirit. Well, to me that was sometimes debatable, but on this day, there was absolutely no room for debate. If I had never felt it before, I felt it then.

"Praise the Lord, saints! This is the day that the Lord has made and I will rejoice and be glad in it! I am so glad to have my friends from The 15th Street Church of The Pentecost here to join us in celebration today, and I'm told that they have with them a young sister with the voice of an angel. Her name is Sister Pleasure Trenton and I want you all to help me welcome her to the choir stand right now to bless us with a song." Bishop Fletcher said as the congregation clapped politely. My mother hugged Pleasure and sent her up to the choir stand for her solo.

The audience was completely silent at first after their applause. And then they began to whisper and rustle in the seats as Pleasure sashayed her way out the microphone in her almost flesh tight too little sweater dress that had everybody's temperature raising.

But the whole church quickly got as quiet as a dead church mouse when Pleasure sat down at the piano and began to play. She had full command of every ear as she again masterfully manipulated the ivory keys. And then she started to sing.

"*Yes, Jesus loves me!... Yes, Jesus loves me! Yes, Jesus loves me. For the bible... Tells... me so!*" Pleasure voice was as smooth as silk. She closed her eyes and sang as if there was nobody else in the church but her God. And then one after another it happened. There was a shout, then another and then another that was even louder than the one before. The sisters in the church began to jump and scream as if they had been attacked by a swarm of honey bees. But there were no bees. It was the Holy Ghost! And before I knew it, just about everyone had it, everybody but me anyway. I wanted to feel it but the spirit never touched me.

This went on for like twenty minutes. I looked around in curious amazement. People were laid out on the floor shaking and crying and thrashing around. There were ushers and nurses holding and restraining people to keep them from hurting themselves.

"This is the holy ghost? But why would God make anybody fall out and act like this?" I asked my mother.

"Hush girl! Don't ever question the Holy Spirit! This is God showing his power. Now, sit back and be quiet!" She said as just about everybody in the church lost control. But all that shoutin' and dancin' and whoopin' and hollerin' was making me nervous, and when I got nervous I had to pee!

So, I quietly eased out of the main sanctuary and headed to the restroom, which was located downstairs near the Sunday school classroom and the Pastor's study.

It was dark, all except for a small speck of light that peeked from underneath the bathroom door that guided me as I felt my way along the wall. I had to go so bad that I was doing the pee-pee dance. I barely got my panties down in enough time.

I sat there for a moment listening to everybody still stomping, dancing and shouting to the praise music right up above my head. I thought the ceiling would fall in. And then I heard strange noises coming from the other side of the wall where the pastor's study was.

So, I finished using the toilet, washed my hands, but there were no towels to dry them.

Then, I opened the door and started to walk back up stairs. But I heard I the strange noise again coming from the pastor's study. It sounded like someone was crying. So I went over to the door slowly and stood, as the crying got louder. But it wasn't really crying. It sounded more like who ever it was, was sick or in some kind of pain. So I opened the door.

And there was Sister Givens, one of the church nurses bent over the big cherry wood desk with her skirt pulled up and her top hanging off her shoulders, exposing her bare breasts. "Oh God yes! Fuck me! Aww shit, that's it! I'm cummin'! This is yo' pussy! Fuck me! I'm cummin! There it is! Right there, Eldon! Yes! Yes!" She screamed in a partially contained whisper. And behind her, huffing and puffing like the big bad wolf, with his pants down around his ankles and his face dripping with sweat was Bishop Fletcher.

They both quickly stopped and turned to look at me as I stood like a deer in the headlights. Then the bishop lunged over the desk toward me, with his pants still down around his ankles. I screamed & ran straight up the stairs as fast as I could and rushed back into the main sanctuary with my mother who was waiting with our jackets in her arms.

"You ready baby? ... What's wrong? You look like you just seen a ghost? Are you alright?" She asked, as I stood trembling, and ashamed of what I had just seen. Pleasure stood next to my mother with a puzzled look on her face.

"Hey, girl. You missed the last part of my solo. What took you so long?" Pleasure asked as Sister Fletcher came over and hugged her and my mother and me.

"Thank y'all for comin'! Angell yo' little friend is very talented. I want y'all to say hi to Bishop. Now, I wonder where he could be? I coulda'' swore I just saw him! Have you seen him Angell?" Asked Sister Fletcher. She was head of the music ministry and she was also Bishop Fletcher's wife.

"Umm... Well... I... Uh... " I stuttered as I held my head down, trying to think of something to say without lying or getting caught up in any mess.

"Child, did you hear Sister Fletcher talkin' to you", my mother said looking at me oddly.

"Oh, never mind here he comes now. Eldon, come over here and say hi!" Sister Fletcher shouted and motioned for the pastor to come over where we were standing. I stood perfectly still with my eyes still trained on the floor.

"Eldon, this is Pleasure! She's lil' Angell's friend... (Sister Fletcher paused) "What is that? Eldon, you smell kinda' funny" Sister Fletcher said as she leaned over and sniffed the bishop.

"What? Oh, it's nothing! I was just downstairs... The toilet was acting up again in the men's bathroom. So, I, uh... (The bishop stuttered) "Hello Angell. Nice seeing you again." Bishop Fletcher said as he peered at me from the corner of his bad eye as if he was waiting on me to tell what I saw him doing with that stank lady down in the basement.

"Anyway, we thank y'all for comin' out! And we definitely got to start getting together more." Sister Fletcher said as she again hugged my mother and kissed both Pleasure and me on the cheek.

"Yeah. We'll get together soon. Come on Dear. Let's go say goodbye to the Miltons" Bishop said as he grabbed Sister Eldon by the hand and quickly drug her away.

At that exact moment, the skank nurse that had been downstairs with bishop getting hit from the back walked by and gave us a very fake hello.

"Praise the Lord, Sister Epps!" she said as she switched past smellin' like a day old fish dinner.

"Y'all smell that? Hmm... She musta' been downstairs workin' on that toilet too." My mother said sarcastically as I looked at Pleasure and busted out laughing.

"Girl, what's so funny?" Pleasure asked.

"Nothin' girl. I'll tell you when we get back on the van. I promise! But you gotta promise not to say a word to anybody, not even your granny" I said to Pleasure as we all made our way back outside.

When we got back on the van I told Pleasure what happened in the downstairs of the church. She couldn't believe it. And to tell you the truth, I could hardly believe it myself. It was all we could do keep ourselves under control. Pleasure and I both about fell out of our seats laughing the whole way back to Liberty City. And then just as we hit 15th, the smiles quickly left our faces.

Bright flashing lights and sirens met us about two blocks away from the house. There were three police cars, two fire trucks and an ambulance that just about took up the entire street. And the smell of smoke filled the air as a policeman approached the van and motioned for my father to roll the window down. We all instantly started to choke.

"This street is gonna be blocked off for a while. There was an explosion in that old house next to the church." The officer said as he walked away, swiftly heading back in the direction of Pleasure's house.

"Wait! Did you say that there was an explosion?" My father yelled back out at the officer.

"Yeah! The fire fighters just pulled an old lady out and put her into the ambulance. It's damn shamed too. The fire marshal was just here a few weeks ago, trying to warn her about the faulty wiring in the house. I guess she wasn't able to get it fixed.

Anyway, the coroner should be here in a minute!" The officer responded as we all looked at each other in horror. And then... Pleasure began to scream.

"Granny! Granny! Let me out! I gotta go see what happened to my granny! Open the door! Open the door!" Pleasure shouted as she tried to get out of the church van. My mother grabbed Pleasure and struggled to restrain her.

As the fire fighters began to gain control over the fire, we were able to get a better look at what was going on. Pleasure's house was totally engulfed in flames. A thick cloud of smoke and ash drifted for blocks. The whole front of the house had been blown to bits, and the pieces were scattered everywhere.

Pleasure kicked and screamed as the ambulance whizzed by with its lights flashing and the sirens screeching.

My father quickly backed the van out and hit a u-turn, as we quickly made our way over to Jackson Memorial, which was just about five minutes away.

"No! No! No! I want my Granny! Please! Take me to my Granny! She can't be dead! She just can't be!" Pleasure sobbed and screamed in agony as my father sped down the street, right behind the ambulance.

My father opened the van and got out and met one of the paramedics.

"How is she? How is the old lady? She's okay, ain't she?" My father asked as the paramedics opened the doors to the ambulance and pulled out the stretcher with a white sheet completely covering the lifeless body of Pleasure's grandma.

"I'm sorry. She didn't make it. She was killed instantly by the blast. The police think it must have been some kind of gas explosion. She never stood a chance. I'm sorry! We'll need someone to come and identify the body for the coroner. I'm sorry again." The paramedic said as Pleasure jumped up and down, and began screaming in unimaginable grief. My father followed the paramedics inside.

Pleasure fell down on the curb and cried out. "God! Why? Why do you hate me? First you took my father, and then my mother. And now you're takin' my Granny? Why God? Please just tell me why! Why don't you love me? Why even allow me to be born, if all I would ever be meant to do is suffer?"

My mother held Pleasure close and rocked her in her arms like a baby. And I began to pray inside myself. I began to ask God why. Why would he allow an innocent of old woman to be killed? Why would he allow a young girl with nobody else in the world to turn to, to become orphaned and alone? Her grandma was the only person she had left that cared anything about her. What was she gonna do now? Where was she gonna go?

Only God knew.

CHAPTER 6

After my father came from inside the hospital, we got back in the van and made the drive back home. It was the longest, quietest, and saddest trip I ever made.

We only lived about five minutes away, but it felt like we had been in that van for hours. And the closer we got to home the more my stomach started to hurt. Because I knew that we had to go back and see the scene of the explosion that took Ms. Trenton's life. And even worse, I knew that Pleasure would have to see it. I knew that this would be the hardest pill to swallow, for all of us.

As we neared our section of the street the smell of smoke grew stronger. Pleasure began to weep deeply. My father pulled in and parked the van along side our house. Everybody was still standing around on the block retelling the story of the blast, still crying and shaking their heads in disbelief.

Everyone stared with pity and pointed as we got out of the van and rushed inside to spare Pleasure from having to witness the burned out, smoldering mess any longer than she had to. All the neighbors looked on in curiosity. Even the local hustlas stopped to observe. And Pleasure's nigga Boom-Boom stood mixed into the background, barely visible, but he was there. Pleasure stopped slightly as they locked eyes from a distance. My parents didn't seem to notice her distraction but I did.

That night, Pleasure and I sat in the quiet darkness of my room on the edge of the bed. We stared together out of the window at the smoky rubble that just a few short hours before was the place that and her grandmother called home. Now Pleasure didn't have a grandmother or a home. Her teardrops fell silently, but I heard each one hit the window seal as I sat next to her and held her hand.

"Well, Pleasure. It's pretty late. Maybe we should say our prayers and try to get some sleep." I said as I stood slowly and leaned on the bedpost.

"Prayers? You must be crazy! I ain't never speakin' to God again. He don't care about me. He couldn't possibly care about me. So, I don't care about him either. My granny was always talkin' about the love of God and how much he cares for us. She loved God, but he let her die.

He didn't care about her. My granny was a good woman, a real good woman! And if he didn't care nothin' about her, then I know he don't care nothin' about me." Pleasure said as she began to almost hyperventilate with grievous tears.

"Pleasure, God loves you! He loves all of us!" I replied as I sat back down next to her on the bed and touched her shoulder to comfort her.

"That's easy for you to say! You still have a mother and a father. I don't have anything or anybody. I am alone. I don't even have any clothes. Everything I had is gone! Everything!" Pleasure said as she began to weep inconsolably.

"Pleasure, you're wrong. You're not alone. And God does love you and so do we." My mother said as she opened the door and entered the room with the bright light from the hallway shining from behind her, a light that gave her an almost angelic appearance.

"You don't even know me! How can you say that you love me? That's just some more of that phony church talk. That's just some fake stuff that church folks say." Pleasure said as she buried her face in a pillow. Then my mother came, sat down next to Pleasure and laid her hands on her back as she began to softly pray out loud.

My mother sat up all that night and held Pleasure's hand as she cried herself to sleep. I curled up on the other side of the bed and watched mother try to consol Pleasure in vain.

My father stood quietly and anonymously outside the doorway of my room and listened for a while. He never said a word but I knew that he was out there. He wasn't much for words; my father was one of those kinds of men that really didn't need words to express the way he was feeling. Most times his actions told it all. And just like my mother, I knew that he was feeling Pleasure's grief, but in a strangely different way.

I don't think that any of us got any real sleep that night. We all just sort of closed our eyes because our eyes were tired and trouble was heavy on our minds. But that night, there was no real rest for the weary.

When I woke up in the morning, I tried to be as still as possible so as not to disturb Pleasure. I laid still. I could hear my parents downstairs in the kitchen talking. The heat vent by my bed carried their voices up in to my room like a bootleg intercom.

They were talking about what happened to Mrs. Trenton and how terrible it was. They were also talking about how Pleasure didn't have any relatives to go to. And mother said that she was not about to see Pleasure go to any orphanage or foster home, or be turned out into the streets. And my father agreed.

They both decided that they needed to go to the people at the welfare and petition for emergency custody of Pleasure so that she could legally stay with us in our home and not be taken away by the county or something.

So my mother made a few calls to some of the caseworkers she knew and got a temporary court order that would allow Pleasure to stay with us.

When Pleasure awoke, she got up, walked over to the window, paused a second and began to weep all over again. I didn't know what to say, so, I didn't say anything. I just waited until she was ready to talk. But I would wait the entire week without almost any communication from her at all.

That week Pleasure and I were suppose to had started school, but my mother decided that because of everything that had happened it might be better if she home schooled us, at least for while anyway.

I was so disappointed! This was supposed to be the year that I got to school with the other kids. All summer long I had been so excited, it was all that I thought about. But my mother thought it would be best for Pleasure if we both were taught together. We were both going to the seventh grade, so, we would have probably had a lot of the same classes anyway.

The next seven days were pretty rough. We did everything that we possibly could to help Pleasure get through, but sometimes the only cure for hurt is time. And sometimes, even time can't erase the pain. But time goes on.

On that very next Monday we laid Pleasure's grandmother to rest. My father preached at the funeral and my mother gave the eulogy. Her grandma didn't have any friends or family there besides Pleasure, but her service was packed with a lot of people from the community.

Everybody from Liberty City came to pay their respects, even Boom-Boom and his bother Big-Mann came and brought flowers. The members of his cartel stood in the back of the church with dark shades on. Pleasure's grandma had to be turning in her grave at their very sight.

Pleasure sat at the very front of the church with me and my mother. She cried a river of tears that seemed as if they would never end, and at the last part of the funeral service my father asked Pleasure if there was anything that she wanted to say. Pleasure stood to her feet without saying a word, walked over to her grandmother's casket and started to sing. All the sisters in the church started to scream and shout with the Holy-Ghost. I looked around and shook my head at the spectacle.

When peace like a river attends my way. When sorrow like sea billows roll. Whatever my lot thou haste taught me to say. It is well; it is well with my soul.

"That was my grandmother's favorite song. Thank everyone for coming" Pleasure said. The whole church was moved to tears.

As we all moved out of the church to go to the cemetery for the burial, Big Mann and his cartel stood off to the side next to three brand new shiny Mercedes Benz's. Dark shaded lenses coved their eyes, but it was obvious that they were watching Pleasure. Boom Boom's mouth almost began to water at the sight of her sweet, tender curves.
"I gotta have some of that. And I ain't tryin' to wait too long either!' Boom-Boom said to Big Mann.

"Easy, Lil bro' Just chill! Patience is a virtue. Pleasure comes to those who wait! Ha! Ha! Ha!" Big Mann responded to this little brother as they both rudely laughed out loud, leaning against Big Mann's fly whip with the 22-inch chrome wheels.

I slightly paused and looked over at Big-Mann, causing the two disorderly thugs to briefly straighten up, as we passed walking behind the pallbearers who carried the casket. My mother, my father, and me and Pleasure all got into the funeral car with the black tinted windows. The whole block was filled with people. We could barely get through the crowd.

Pleasure stared blankly out of the window as we made our way to the cemetery. She really hadn't said much of anything since her grandma died. I guess she was still in shock & I guess I couldn't blame her. I had not felt the bitter sting of death since my grandpa passed away, but that was a long time ago, and I was just a little girl then. Now I was starting to see life from a totally different prospective. I was starting to see that prayer didn't always fix everything right away, like my mother told me it would. But we still kept right on praying.

The weeks that followed were really rough for the whole family. My mother and father were doing everything that they possibly could to help Pleasure get through her loss.

Since she had lost pretty much everything that she had in the fire, so my parents went out and bought her all new shoes and clothes, but they couldn't replace her memories. Only God and time could repair that.

During the day we would study with my mother. She taught us English, math, science and world studies. In the afternoons after about four hours of lessons, my mother would give us a break. And she would usually go have prayer with Sister Walls. Me & Pleasure would have our lunch and just kind of chill out for about an hour or two and just talk.

Then after lunch we would have bible study. My mother would pick a scripture and ask us to tell her what we thought it meant. Pleasure would just get really quiet. My mother could never get Pleasure to participate in any discussions that pertained to religion. And I knew why.

Pleasure was mad at God. She believed that if God really loved her that he would never have allowed all the bad things that happened in her life to have taken place. Her heart was broken.

And it seemed that there was only one thing that really made Pleasure happy and that was music. Sometimes she would sit by herself for hours and play the piano. She also sang in the choir on Sundays. She didn't really want to do it at first, but she did it to please my mother. And because of that Pleasure was actually gaining quite a lot of attention for her singing. People from all over Miami had started to take notice. Pleasure was becoming a little celebrity.

Pleasure had started to develop a reputation as a great singer. One person that had become really interested in her singing was Big-Mann.

He was known as a notorious businessman, some even called him a gangster, but he had recently joined our church, and turned his life over to Jesus Christ. And now he was determined to make his mark in the gospel music business. He had also decided that he was going to help Pleasure take her music to the next level.

Big-Mann had found Jesus, but he was still a shrewd businessman, and he knew a money making opportunity when he saw it.

Big-Mann was about to start Miami's largest, independent gospel music label and he wanted Pleasure as his first artist. He said that she would set the world of gospel music on fire. Pleasure sure had the talent to do it and Big-Mann had the means to make it happen.

But there was just one problem. Before he could turn Pleasure into the next gospel music superstar, he had to get past my mother and father, who both knew his former reputation as a dangerous crime boss. And I knew that even though he claimed to be a born again Christian, there was no way on God's green earth that my parents would ever let Pleasure get involved with Big Mann. But he always had a way of getting what he wanted, because he wasn't just some dope-boy selling nickel bumps in front of the projects, Big-mann was a kingpin!

CHAPTER 7

It was about six o'clock on a Thursday night. We were all just about to sit down to dinner. My mother had just finished making the lemonade. Me and Pleasure were in the dining room setting the table. My father was in the living room watching the news when the doorbell rang.

My mother wiped her hands and hurried into the living room to see who it was. She opened the door and paused.

"Can I help you?" She said to the large, well-dressed man wearing a dark blue Italian made three-piece suit, with matching alligator shoes.

"Good evening! Is the pastor home?" The man replied with a wide toothy grin. "I'm Tony Mann, Big-Mann. I'm Elizabeth Mann's grandson. I just joined the church a few weeks ago", he added.

"I know exactly who you are but, what can we do for you?" My mother asked curtly.

"It's okay, Honey" My father said as he got up from the couch and walked over to the door.

"Well, well, well! Good evening Pastor. Just thought I'd stop by and say hello. How's everything?" Big-Mann asked with all thirty-two of his big, yellow, cigar stained teeth still showing.

"Everything is fine Tony. In fact, we were all just about to sit down to dinner", my father said apprehensively as Big-Mann looked over his shoulder at me and Pleasure.

"Well, I won't take up too much of your time" (He paused) "Hello young ladies! You two are just getting more and more beautiful everyday. Pleasure, I was so sorry to hear about your grandmother. She was a real nice lady, a good Christian woman! That's kind of the reason I'm here. May I come in for a second? It's kinda windy out here", he said as he stood at the entrance of the doorway

Big-Mann was a huge, menacing figure, with a deep scratchy voice. He stood every bit of 6'6 and 350 pounds. He kinda' put you in the mind of Suge Knight, but only bigger and way scarier looking. His Armani cologne filled the living room as he stepped in with his bodyguard right behind.

"Girl, you got quite voice on you, you sing like an angel." Big-Mann said as he looked at Pleasure, with dollar signs in his eyes.

"I guess I sound okay." Pleasure said.

"Your voice is incredible and I'm just gonna get to the point. I think you have some real talent. I heard you sing at your grandma funeral and it literally brought me to tears" Big-Mann said, touching his chest with fake sincerity.

"Pleasure, I'm starting a brand new gospel record label. And I want you to be my first solo artist. This is gonna be big! Bigger than Motown! I also wanna give you this. (Big-Mann reached into his jacket pocket and pulled out an envelope) It's just a small gift to help you out. I understand that you don't have any family here and that you pretty much lost everything in that fire. Maybe this will help out a little", Big-Mann said as he handed Pleasure a cashier's check for $5000.

It's a gift, whether you sign with my label or not. I still wanna help you. I've already talked to the pastor, and he was really excited about it."

Big-Mann said as he looked over at my father, still cheezin' like a fat rat.

My father stood quietly to the side, leaning against the banister to the stairs.

"You already talked it over with the pastor?" My mother remarked as she walked over to my father and stood in front of him, looking him square in the eye.

"We'd like to get started as soon as possible. The pastor has my number. Good evening again", Big-Mann said as he put his hat back on his big shinny baldhead, and walked out of the door with his bodyguard.

I began to jump up and down, screaming as I put my arms around Pleasure, hugging her with excitement and joy.

"Girl, you about to be a star! I'm so happy for you! You gotta let me fix yo' hair and we got to start looking through some catalogs to find you the right outfits. You gotta have yo' look down packed. You can't be on T.V. singin' for the Lord, looking all plain and shabby!" I shouted excitedly.   My mother snapped her fingers.

"Y'all go upstairs! I wanna talk to the pastor alone for a minute before dinner", my mother said as she stared angrily at my father.

Are you outta your mind? That man is the biggest gangster in Miami! I know you ain't considering lettin' that girl do nothin' with him!", she whispered angrily as me and Pleasure stood at the top of the stairs with our ears to the corner tryin to listen.

"Sarah, give the man a brake. He just got saved and gave his life to Jesus. Look, it's gonna be a gospel music label and I'll be there to over see everything. It's a great opportunity for Pleasure and for the church. Just trust me. Let's just try it out and see where it goes. I've never let you down before, and I 'won't start now", my father said as he put his arms around my mother and kissed her on the cheek.

"Okay, but the minute she starts gettin' behind in her studies or start actin' up, I'm pullin' the plug! (she walked away from father) "Girls, come down and eat!!" She said as Pleasure and I ran down the stairs screaming, overjoyed at what we had just heard.

Along with starting her career in music, that year was also about the time that Pleasure really became involved with Big Mann's little brother Boom-Boom. But she made me swear not to tell a soul.

I think my parents suspected that Pleasure was messin' wit' Boom-Boom because he was always around but he was also Big-Mann's little brother, so they couldn't really prove it. They just sort of figured that he was part of Big Mann's entourage.

So anyway, the next day, Pleasure and I were with my mother in the kitchen going over our studies when we heard all this noise coming from outside. It was a construction crew. They had come with a bulldozer and two dump trucks to tear down what was left of Pleasure's house next door.

Pleasure stood at the screen door that faced out toward the old house and began to cry. She ran upstairs to our room and didn't come back out until it was time for dinner.

The city had ordered that the land be cleared due to pubic health and safety regulations. I was glad to see it go, it was just an ugly reminder of the terrible accident that killed Pleasure's grandma. The City Planning Commission was buying up the whole block.

They even bought the church land. We ended up moving to a really nice neighbor in Miramar, where the new church was going to be built.

A lot happened that year. Big-Mann started Christ's Song Records and they started recording Pleasure's first album. He promoted her as "Miami's Little Angel". On the weekends she would perform at different music events that my father and Big-Mann put together. She made appearances at Gospel-Fest, Spirit-Song and even The Bobby Jones Gospel Show on B.E.T. (Pleasure was an overnight success)

That year Pleasure also became a permanent part of our family after my mother and father legally adopted her. We were all so happy. Pleasure and I had become really close. She had become the sister that I had always wished for. And just like that there she was. We did everything together and kept each other's secrets. Well, it was usually me keeping her secrets, because I really didn't have any secrets for her to keep, except for the fact that I stuffed my bra with tissue. But the secrets that I kept for her were way more juicy!

Like the time my mother and father went away overnight on a church retreat. The night they left, Pleasure invited Boom-Boom over to the house to watch movies. I told her that I was going to bed early, to give them a little privacy, but what I really meant was that I was going to my room and peek out of the door, and watch every move they made. I didn't have a boyfriend or anything else exciting going on. So I sure wasn't about to pass up the chance see what Pleasure and her little thug were about to get into.

Boom-Boom sat on the couch in the living room in clear view of my spying eye. Pleasure turned off the TV and stood in front of it wearing a short white, see through nighty. She grabbed the remote and turned the stereo up loud. She turned the lights down low and moved slowly toward Boom-Boom.

Pleasure leaned in close and whispered something into his ear. He smiled and leaned forward to take his shirt off. Pleasure got on top of him and straddled his lap. They started to kiss wildly. His hands were all over her body, underneath her tiny, sheer nighty.

My hands started to sweat as I held on tightly to the doorknob. I wanted to scream into the living room and tell them to stop, but I was so caught up in what I was seeing that I literally could not move.

My mouth became dry as the desert. Pleasure whispered something again into Boom's ear as she moved from his lap. They both looked back at the door where I was standing. I instantly stopped breathing. I thought I was busted. But I wasn't, they were just looking back to make sure that the door was closed.

I breathed a quiet sigh of relief, pressed my eye back up against the narrow opening of the doorway, took a deep breath and put my fingers down inside my panties to play with my clitoris while I watched. I knew it was wrong, but I couldn't help myself.

Pleasure stood still in the center of the living room as Boom-Boom moved toward her. The muscles from his hard chiseled body seemed to glow against the dim shimmering lights.

Pleasure pushed her thick, wavy hair back out of her face. Boom grabbed her by the waist and snatched her close to him. He kissed her neck and she moaned softly as he gripped her juicy bottom with his rough hands.

He ran his fingers up along her thick thighs, lifting Pleasure's nighty up and over her head.

She was completely naked. And though the light in the room was somewhat weak, I could clearly see everything that was happening.

Boom-Boom leaned in and started to suck on her neck and chest, and then he moved down. She grabbed his neck and threw her head back. "Damn girl, you got a bad ass body," he said as he licked her full, round breast and slid his finger inside her. Pleasure moaned out load.

Boom picked her up off her feet. She wrapped her legs around him as he undid his pants with one hand and held her up in the air by her waist with the other hand.

His pants fell to the floor as he reached down, and pushed himself deep inside her. She screamed over the music as he rocked her to the beat of L.L. Cool J (Around The Way Girl). He held her by both thighs and sexed her in mid-air.

He walked over and laid her down on the sofa. I could see the silhouette of his manhood as he stood over her. it was long and hard, like the tusk of an African elephant.

He laid down between her legs. She gasped. Boom-Boom began to stroke Pleasure like only a real thug could. And it must have been either really, really good or really, really bad, because she holla'd nonstop for almost twenty-five minutes. For a moment I imagined myself laying there in her place, with that vicious thug inside me. I could almost feel his sweaty golden skin sticking to mine. I lost my breath.

When he got up she was shaking all over, he was struggling for air like he had just run the miracle mile, and my panties were soaked straight through. I had never seen anything like that before, not even on TV.

I caught my breath, quietly pushed the door closed and hurried over to the window by my bed, I opened it and stuck my head out to get some air. Then I pulled the covers back on my bed to lay down. But, before I knew what hit me I was crying, I felt so guilty for what I had just done, and for what I had allowed Pleasure to do.

The following day I was so ashamed that I could hardly look at Pleasure. I couldn't even bring myself to tell her what I had seen her doing with Boom. I never brought it up and I never discussed what I saw or did that night, not with anyone.

About a week later, Pleasure asked me to go with her to the free clinic in Liberty City. She said that she hadn't been feeling well. I didn't even ask any questions, like, *why if she didn't feel well, didn't she just tell my mother? And why was she going to the free clinic when we had a family doctor?* I didn't even ask any questions because I figured it must have had something to do with Boom-Boom. And I was right. The doctor at the clinic told Pleasure that she had gonorrhea.

She was so upset and embarrassed. She made me promise on my grandfather's grave that I would never tell a soul. I promised, and kept her secret.

CHAPTER 8

The next four years seemed to just fly by. Pleasure had become quite a huge star in gospel music. My father's church had expanded, becoming the largest worship center in Miami, holding over 15,000 members. And by this time, Pleasure and I were both seniors in high school.

We were both growing up. She had just turned 18 and my 18th birthday was only three months away. But I still looked like a little girl while Pleasure looked like a beautiful, full-grown woman, with big breast, hips and an ass that would make J-Lo go back to her plastic surgeon and demand a refund. Pleasure was cold!

Sometimes it was so crazy being places with her, and having guys look right past me, not only because she was like a celebrity, but mainly because she was drop dead gorgeous, with a body like **whoa**. Usually most guys didn't even realize who she was until they got close up on her. All they really noticed at first would be her curves, and she loved it. Even though she would usually pretend like she didn't.

I use to feel so self-conscious standing next to her. I felt like I had no sex appeal at all. But Pleasure would always tell me "*Just be patient girl, yours is coming!*" But, it felt like it was taking forever. I was almost grown and still built like an eighth grader. In fact some seventh grade girls even had bigger breasts than I did.

But, I was smart and nobody could take that away from me. I got straight A's in all my classes. But nobody really seemed to notice my accomplishments. Even my mother and father seemed to make more of a fuss over Pleasure than they did me. I know they didn't mean to, but they did. It was always, "*Pleasure did this or Pleasure did that*", "*Pleasure's going to be on this T.V show or Pleasure is going to be on that T.V. show.*" "*Pleasure got this award or got that award*". No one really seemed to notice me, except as Pleasure's little sister or "that dark skinned chick" that was always with Pleasure Trenton.

I mean, don't get me wrong. I loved Pleasure and I was happy for all of her success. I was just getting a little sick of being in her shadow. That was until Vartan Daniels and I started going out.

Vartan seemed to grow up overnight and changed from that annoying little boy that carried around the football everywhere he went, to the sexiest boy at school that every girl wanted to get with. He was also the quarterback and captain of the high school football team. He had his pick of any girl he wanted but he wanted me. Those cheerleaders that hung out with the football team hated me. They called me "the beast" and they called him "beauty". And he was beautiful!

He was tall, light skinned with soft-brown eyes and beautiful long dreadlocks that he had been growing since he was six years old. And he had muscles on top of muscles. The word fine did not do him enough justice. It's so odd how I never noticed him before.

Vartan had started trying to talk to me when we were kids, but I was so into my books and church that I never paid it any attention. All I knew was that he always wanted to walk me home after school. And besides that, in my eyes he was still just little dread head Vartan. But boy did he change, and I couldn't deny it.

That year my mother decided to let Pleasure and I attend regular school, so that we could graduate with the other kids from our neighborhood. Vartan was also in our graduating class.

Vartan was really fine and he knew it. But I wasn't going let that phase me the way it did those other girls at our school. You should have seen the way they threw themselves at him, the way they went out of their way to make simple conversation with him. It was shameful. I mean, just because he was captain of the football team and he was cute, with the body of a Greek god meant nothing to me. Okay…. I'm lying! But I wasn't about to let him know how weak he made me. He use to tell me *"you'll give in eventually"* and he was right.

So one day I let him walk me home. I guess that's where it all started. The nerd and the football star. Vartan told me that our relationship was very different from any that he had in the past. He told me that I was special, nothing like the others before me. What he probably meant was, I was the first girl he dated that wasn't givin' it up. I let him know from day one, that I was a virgin and I was staying that way until I got married.

Pleasure said that was the only reason he stayed around, because I never gave it up. She also told me that I was a fool. She believed that if I wasn't giving it to him, that he had to be getting it from somewhere. No man could go that long with out sex, combined with the fact the he was a star athlete and could basically have any girl he wanted. She said that we wouldn't last three months. But she was wrong. We ended up going together four years, and then we got engaged.

We both ended up going to the University of Miami, Vartan was voted MVP and was drafted all pro by the Miami Maxx. He made starting quarter back his first year. He was the man! But he still wasn't getting any until we got married. I didn't care how much money he had or who he played for. That made him so mad sometimes but I told him that if he loved me, he would wait. And he waited.

So while he was setting the football field on fire, I went and earned my teaching degree. That was always my dream, to help kids expand their minds. There were so many people in the ghetto where we were from just wasting their lives, warping their brains with drugs and alcohol, but I felt like if I could just change one life or keep one kid from messing up their future, then my life would have counted for something. I knew that this is what I wanted to do with my life.

Vartan's grandmother went to our church. She was actually one of the oldest members. She was there when my grandfather started pastoring forty-two years ago. Of course that was before we went and got all fancy, and expanded the church to 15,000 members. The new build was so beautiful, but the people in the neighborhood that we came from were still poor and living at the bottom of society's barrel. It was so depressing.
Even though we didn't live in Overtown anymore, me and my mother still did a lot of work in the community, but she was getting older and her health was starting to fail. I didn't find out that she was sick for a while, because she kept it a secret.

Vartan use to volunteer sometimes with kids at the church, but I think it was really more for the publicity. He could be a really arrogant, pompous jerk sometimes, with his football stories and his cars and his money. And it really ticked me off to know that he using those kids to make himself look good.

He had started a program for at risk youth that was sponsored by the football league. Vartan was once an at risk youth himself. He was from those same streets. So, he understood what the kids were up against. He dealt with the peer pressure, the threat of gang violence, and the hopelessness that they saw everyday.

He also had his brushes with the law, getting caught making weed, under-aged drinking, you name it. He even once got caught with a gun. But that was in his younger days. And because of his extra-ordinary talent on the football field, he was always able to got out of whatever trouble that he managed to get into. He was the typical star athlete skating through on his talent. But I use to tell him that one day he was gonna get himself into some kind of trouble that his talent couldn't get him out of.

But he had grown into a different person, sort of. I mean he was still loud and arrogant at times, but for the most part, he was a pretty okay guy. And the fact that he stood by me patiently for five years and respected my decision to keep my virginity until I got married meant so much to me.

But Pleasure was convinced that no man could be faithful to a virgin and go without sex for that long. She seemed convinced that Vartan was creepin' on me, but I believed in him.

CHAPTER 9

So while Pleasure was making a name for herself in the world of gospel music and Vartan was gettin' his MVP on, I was doing my thing, working with the kids from the inner city.

I had gotten a position as a high school math teacher at Miami North Western High School in the old neighborhood we use to live in. That's where I met Chance. He was an art teacher and he helped out with the after school program that served mostly latch key kids whose parents worked in the evenings or that just didn't feel like being bothered with 'em.

Chance was a wonderful teacher, very patient and understanding. All the kids loved him. He seemed to really identify with where they were coming from. He always listened and talked to them, not at them. And I really appreciated having somebody that listened to me too.

Chance had a really different way about himself. He was very quiet, almost kind of shy. But when he spoke, he commanded a respect that I had rarely seen anyone get, especially from those inner city kids. Some of them were pretty tough; they had to be, because where they lived, only the strong survived.

I use to stay late after school three or four nights a week. Chance would be there with the kids helping them with art projects or tutoring some of them with homework. His class was right across from mine. I could see his desk from where I sat.

Some nights when I got finished with my lesson plans, I would just sit and watch him. He was so tall and handsome, very neat and well put together. His physique was slim, but very muscular and he had a smooth baldhead. His skin was like dark chocolate and his eyes were a deep brown. His lips were full and beautiful, and seemed to be whispering into me in my ear.

Chance was poetry in motion. He was so different from Vartan. Don't get me wrong. I loved Vartan, but I just didn't like him most of the time. He was so loud and arrogant and Chance was so quiet and modest.

On the nights we worked late together, Chance would always ask if he could walk me to my car and of course I always said yes. I mean after all, Vartan was either busy practicing football or on the road at a game. In fact, I was actually starting to see less and less of him, which was kind of funny since I was really moving into the most difficult phase of my life.

My mother had been diagnosed with stage-four breast cancer and she had only been given a year or so to live. I was crushed.

My mother was my best friend. She taught me everything I knew, how to walk, how to talk, how to act. She instilled in me my faith in God. All that I was and all that I would ever hope to become, I owed to my mother. She was a shining example of what a real woman ought to be. She was a wife, a mother and a friend. I could only hope to be half the woman she was.

My mother was so brave and so strong. She said that she had lived a full life and had done everything she ever wanted to do. She loved a wonderful man, she had a beautiful family and she helped as many people along the way as she could. She was glad that God had blessed her to be a blessing to so many other people and that giving had been her greatest gift.

Cancer is a horrible disease; it actually turns your own body against itself. In a few short months it had ravaged my mother, leaving her almost unrecognizable. It had taken her hair, health and her strength but it couldn't take her spirit.

She was almost as helpless as a baby, unable to do anything for herself. So, I pretty much was with her around the clock when I could be. Pleasure and I alternated in shifts. She would stay with her during the day when I was at work. Then I would come home and tend to her at night.

My mother's body was just a fragmented shell of what it once was. The cancer had metastasized and spread from her breast to her bones, and from her bone it spread to her lungs. And by this time she was in constant pain. She was wasting away.

We had an around the clock hospice nurse there, but I still insisted on always bathing her and changing her when I could. It was my honor, because she had done the same for me as a child. I sat up and held her hand all night, because she would have done the same for me. I sat quietly beside her bed and prayed, because she had done the same for me so many times. To be at her deathbed was my privilege.

During this time I got the opportunity to really know Chance too, we would sit in the teacher's lounge at lunch time and just talk. I would tell him all about Vartan, and my mother and father. With Vartan being away all the time I needed someone to talk to and Chance was there, he was a great listener.

My mother's illness was really hard on all of us. My father was so tired and worn down, between his duties at the church and being worried about my mother that he was starting to come apart himself. The demands of his office as a pastor required that he be away from home a lot. So, not only was my man not able to be there for me when I needed him most, but neither was my father. I would have been totally alone if it wasn't for Pleasure and Chance.

But Pleasure sometimes had trouble expressing her emotions. I knew that she cared about my mother, but I could tell that talking about the way she was feeling made her uncomfortable. My mother was about to be the third mother that Pleasure had lost if you counted her grandma.

When I got home at night sometimes I would hear Pleasure in my mother's room, singing to her. My mother loved church hymns. And singing was actually the only real way that Pleasure was able to express herself sometimes. Her voice was sweet, and her songs comforted my mother.

When my father was home sometimes he would sit in my mother's room with Pleasure while she sang. Over the last couple of years that my mother's health had started failing, my father and Pleasure had become very close. She actually spent more time with him than I did.

Pleasure was one of the most popular members of our church, because she was a very well known gospel music singer. And she would also travel with my father to church conferences and programs around the country.

Big Mann, who was the head of the record label that Pleasure was signed to, had actually put my father in charge of her tour and concert schedule. This was why she often performed at his conferences too. I guess it was his way of also keeping a closer eye on her, since she was like a daughter to him.

My father and Pleasure both disliked Vartan. They both thought that he was all wrong for me. My father also said that he was a lousy quarterback and that the Miami Maxx was a much better team before they drafted him. And for some strange reason he just could not believed that Vartan was faithful to me either, which was kind of funny considering that him and my mother had not had sex in close to three years, according to her. Even before that, she said that they only did it two or three times a year. So my father's theory that a man couldn't go without sex had a few holes in it. I felt like, if he could be faithful to my mother then Vartan could do the same for me.

Besides that, Vartan was a man, and a man is going to do what a man is going to do!

There wasn't a whole lot that I could do about that. Not to mention that Vartan was a professional football player with a lot of money, if he wanted to mess around, it wasn't much I was going to be able to do about it anyway. There was always gonna be some little bobble headed bitch somewhere waiting in the wings to get her hands on my man. So I wasn't about to let that kind of stuff start worrying me. After all, my mother was dying of cancer, and trying to keep up with some nigga was really the least of my concerns.

And purely by accident I had started spending quite a bit of time with Chance. We would eat lunch together a few days a week, plus we both had the same planning period, so sometimes I would go over to his classroom and sit and watch him paint. He was really talented and he fascinated me. He was so different from any guy I had ever met before, especially Vartan.

Chance was so caring and concerned about the kids. He was so in intelligent, and he was focused and sure of himself, not conceited but confident. He didn't need to brag and boast or show off to empress anybody. He reminded me of my favorite bible verse.

1st Corinthians 13:4.

Love is always patient and kind, it is never jealous, love is never boastful or conceited, it is never rude or selfish, it does not take offense and is not resentful. Love takes no pleasure in other's misery but delights in the truth, it's always ready to excuse, to trust and to endure whatever comes. Loves does not come to an end.

CHAPTER 10

The more time I spent with Chance the more I started to really care for him. He started to become apart of my thoughts. I was even starting to find my self fantasizing about him and imaging his touch.

I was having thoughts of him that had never even allowed me to have about Vartan and he was my fiancé. I was way out of order, and I knew it.

One night after school, I had stayed late to grade some papers. Chance was cleaning up after his latch key kids, the last of which had just gone home. He was at the sink in the back of the room washing out some paint brushes. I had come from my classroom and walked into the hall and stood outside his open door.

The evening breeze made its way in through an open window and carried the scent of his cologne over to where I stood. He wore Kenneth Cole cologne. It drove me crazy.

Chance stopped instantly and turned around smiling sensing someone watching him from outside the open door of his classroom, he knew it was me. I was startled and completely embarrassed. I wanted to run away but my legs wouldn't move at all.

He walked over to me, wiping his hands with a paper towel. He stopped & stood in front of me and smiled with the most gorgeous white teeth.

"You scared me", he said, still smiling and penetrating me with his dark brown eyes as I stood paralyzed, knowing that he feared nothing. Fear was not even in his character.

I was speechless, and he knew it.

"Never mind! Lemme walk you to your car", he said as he locked up the room and turned out the lights.

"I didn't drive today, I got dropped off. My sister Pleasure is on her way to pick me up" I said as we walked down the semi-lit hallway, and out to the front of the school.

"Where's your boyfriend tonight?" Chance asked sarcastically.

"You know exactly where he is. He's in Cincinnati, he had a game against the Bengal's." I responded to Chance, placing my hand around his strong muscular arm.

"Well, I'm not much of a football fan!" he said as he laughed lightly.

"Hey. Aren't you from Cincinnati?" I asked.

"Yeah", Chance answered solemnly, as his mind seemed to go to another place in time. Chance was always kind of guarded about his past for some reason. Anytime the subject came up, he would become very quiet and distant, so I never really pressed the issue.

"So anyway, when is the wedding?" Chance said as a light smirk came across his face. "I don't even wanna think about that right now. It's actually the last thing on my mind if you really must know. I mean my mother is dying and all this nigga can do is..." I caught myself as I began to go into a full tirade.

"I'm sorry!" I said as I quickly got a hold of myself.

"No, I'm sorry! I didn't mean to upset you. I was just..." Chance attempted to say as he was cut off by the sound of Pleasure's horn blowing from her new Mercedes Benz SLK. Her stereo was bumpin' the new Keyshia Cole CD.

"Well, I gotta go. I guess I'll see you tomorrow, drive safe. It looks like a storm might be moving this way." I said before pausing and looking away to the other side of the street at someone that appeared to be staring at us but I couldn't see their face because they were wearing a hooded sweat shirt.

"You okay?" Chance asked.

"Yeah, I'm fine." I responded as I looked back across the street but the person that had been staring at us was gone.

"Yeah, okay then. Y'all be safe." Chance said as I got in the car and shut the door. I turned down the deafening music. I love me some Keyshia Cole too, but I wasn't about to let her bust my eardrums.

"Oou wee, girl! Was that Chance? Or do I even need to ask? That has got to be him!" Pleasure said as she sat there for a moment in neutral staring at Chance, almost foaming at the mouth.

"Yeah. That's Chance." I responded, looking back at him, almost foaming at the mouth myself. As Chance started to walk away Pleasure punched the clutch and burned rubber speeding down NW 71st; sometimes she could be so hood!

Chance turned around and watched us as we headed toward I-95.

"Oh! Sweet Jesus! That boy is fine! No wonder!" Pleasure shouted as if she had been touched by the Holy Ghost, but there was nothing holy about what she was thinking.

"No wonder, what?" I responded quickly.

"No wonder you talk about him all the time. He is too cute!" she commented.

"I do not talk about Chance all the time! He is just someone I work with, end of story! Now, how is momma?" I asked after immediately changing the subject.

"She's fine. She's there with the nurse, and Sister Walls is there too. Look, I was thinking, why don't we take the night off and go have ourselves a nice dinner on South Beach. We can have a couple of drinks and chill out. Let's try and get our minds off things for a while. You could use a break!" Pleasure said as she headed in the direction of South Beach.

"I don't know! I don't wanna leave momma alone like that!" I responded.

"She'll be fine and it'll just be for a couple of hours. Come on! It'll do us both some good to get out." Pleasure responded.

"And we'll check on her every thirty minutes!" she added.

"Okay. But only for a couple of hours!" I said hesitantly as we approached our favorite restaurant, Joe Stories on the beach.

While we waited to be seated I called home to check on things at the house. Sister walls answered the phone and said that my mother was resting comfortably and had just had her bath and been put to bed. She told me that my father had just gotten home from church and was sitting with my mother in her room, which made me feel a little better.

Sister Walls said that she had been there all day and was about to go home and get some rest herself. But my mother was in good hands with my father and the nurse.

So, I decide to try to take Pleasure's advice and try to relax a little and have a nice dinner. Pleasure was having no problem at all relaxing. She was already at the bar getting her serious flirt on with the sexy Cuban bartender as he mixed her drink.

I was just about to walk over to the bar with Pleasure when I looked out of the side window. There was that same guy I saw earlier across the street from the school. I recognized him because he was wearing the same grey hoodie. I tried, but I still couldn't see his face. Then I heard Pleasure call my name from the bar, I quickly looked over at her and when I turned back around, just like that, the guy in the hoodie was gone again. I thought it was weird, but I shook it off and walked over to the bar next to Pleasure.

"I just called to check on Mama. The nurse said she was resting and my father was there too", I said as I stared at Pleasure sideways.

"Good! See, I told you everything was fine when I left. Stop worrying! Let's just chill and have a little fun. Girl, do you see this bartender? He is as fine as he wanna be! I'm gettin' my holla on tonight! I'm through wit' Boom" Pleasure said as she stuck her finger into the glass of Hennessey she had ordered. She pulled her finger out, and licked it, in full sight of the bartender.

"Yeah right! Where have I heard that before? And why are you actin up? When did you start drinking?" I asked as she teased the bartender with her eyes.

"Girl calm down! It's just Hennessey! You act like I'm in here smoking crack or something! Relax! Oh! Look there's yo' husband on T.V. Opps! He dropped the ball again! What else is new? Let's hope he's better in bed than he is on the football field or you are gonna be one sexually frustrated housewife. But I guess that doesn't matter too much, since sex doesn't really interest you anyway" Pleasure smirked and pointing to the television set that was positioned above the bar, set on ESPN. They were showing the game between the Miami Maxx and the Cincinnati Bengals. As the camera panned across the field and onto the sideline I just about choked on the glass of water I was sipping. There was Dilonda Lovetts, from Liberty City. "But it couldn't be" I thought to myself, trying not let Pleasure see my expression. She hated that girl because she swore up and down that Dilonda was after Vartan. But had already told that she was messin" around with one of the other players from the team. I just didn't feel like hearing Pleasure's mouth. So I decided to distract her with a little friendly argument.

"Well, at least I'm not messin" wit some thugged out street hustla from Overtown! And still getting' up in front of the whole church on Sunday mornings fake, praisin' the Lord!" I fired back rapidly. Most people still had no idea that Pleasure and Boom-Boom were involved, nobody but me. And I never told anybody, not even my mother.

"I'm sorry, Girl! I didn't mean any harm. I was just givin' you a hard time, that's all" Pleasure said as she grabbed my hand, knowing she had really struck a nerve. But I knew how to strike right back.

"It's cool. Hey! Our table is ready. Let's eat! I'm starving!" I said as the waiter motioned for us to followed him over to the table to be seated.

I ordered the Seafood Deluxe. Pleasure had the grilled salmon Florentine. We both had the Baked Alaska for dessert.

Dinner was fabulous and it really did feel good to get out of the house, and get things off my mind. I was able to push everything out, except for the thought of Chance. For some reason, I just could not get him out of my head.

Pleasure talked all-night about her new album. She said that Big-Mann was pressuring her to get back into the studio. But she told him that she needed more time, because of my mother.

He told her that he didn't care about that. He said that her mother was dead, and that there was nothing that she could do for mine. So he wanted her back in the studio in two weeks, period. He said that she had a music career to think about, and that she was affecting his money. And in the end that's all he ever really cared about was his money. I never like that fat bastard anyway!

So, after dinner we paid the bill, which came to $190. And we didn't even have enough left for a to go box. But Pleasure paid for it, so I guess it was okay. I didn't throw money around like that, because technically I was still poor.

I mean, true enough, we lived in a nice home in Miramar and my father now had a brand new Caddy, and Pleasure was rolling around in a new Mercedes Benz, but I was still a school teacher making $45,000 a year. So I drove a car that I could afford and only spent according to my budget.

Vartan tried to buy me a luxury car as an engagement gift. He said that no fiancé of his ought to be ridin' around in a Honda accord, because he had a reputation to up hold and that I was cramping his style. But I explained to him that expensive things didn't impress me. I didn't need a $100,000 car to make me feel special, because I knew that I already was special. I still don't think that he ever really understood.

That night, it was starting to get pretty late, so we headed home. On the way, I decided to call and check on my mother once more and let my father know where we were. But there was no answer, which was kind of strange.

"It is after eleven-thirty! Everybody is probably asleep. At least they were, until yo' happy ass decided to ring every phone in the house. You need to relax, before you bust an artery or somethin", Pleasure said as she turned up the stereo again, about to let Keyshia Cole destroy what was left of my hearing.

The next fifteen minutes were torture on my eardrums. I praised the lord as we approached our sub-division and Pleasure had to cut the stereo down. They didn't play that ghetto stuff around there like they did in Liberty City, it was a $1000 fine for breaking the noise ordinance, and Pleasure had already been cited twice by the police.

As we got to the house everything was calm. All the lights were out. Everybody seemed to be asleep. We both eased in the front door. Pleasure went into the kitchen for a glass of water and I went in to check on my mother.

Quietly, I walked down the hall, stopped at my mother's room, gently turned the knob, and opened the door.

Immediately my blood ran cold. My mother's heart monitor was beeping like crazy. I quickly turned on the lights and ran over to her bed. She wasn't breathing and she had no pulse.

I screamed at the top of my lungs and ran out into the hallway. Pleasure hurried from the kitchen. I told Pleasure to call 911 and go back in the room with my mother. I ran down the hallway in terror looking for my father, knowing that he must have fallen asleep and not heard my mother's heart monitor going off.

I ran up to his door without knocking and turned the knob.

"Daddy, Daddy!" I yelled as I opened the door to find my father on the couch, buttnekket, in between the legs of my mother's nurse. They were going at it like two rabbits.

I was sick. I couldn't speak or catch my breath. I threw up all over the floor.

My father and the nurse scrambled for their clothes. The nurse tried to run out of the room pass me but she slipped and fell in my vomit. I quickly reached out and grabbed her by her hair and slammed her face against the hard marble that was all covered in puke. My father jumped in between us and tried to break it up, so I punched him too. Just then, the paramedics were beating at the front door. Pleasure ran and let them in.

My father started yelling, "What's wrong, Bean Pole? What's wrong? Why are paramedics here?"

Apparently neither my father nor that nasty bitch of a nurse had any idea what was going on. I guess they were both too horny to hear my mother gagging for her last breath. The nurse was so embarrassed that she ran out of the house and left.

The paramedics rushed my mother to the ambulance, and then off to the hospital, I road with them. Pleasure jumped in her Mercedes and sped the whole way. She even beat us there.

CHAPTER 11

The Paramedics worked on my mother the whole way, but there was nothing they could do. It was too late. They said that she had lost too much oxygen. So, the doctors pronounced her dead at 12:16am that morning.

I sat in the emergency room in shock. Finally, Pleasure and my father arrived. They knew my mother was gone. They could tell by the look on my face that she had passed away.

My father began to cry. I walked right up to him and tried to slap the damn taste out of his mouth, Then, I just walked out of the hospital.

Pleasure was completely stunned by my actions, because she didn't get the joy of walking in and seeing him with his dick inside the nurse. So she had no clue. But she ran out side to catch me and I told her what had happened. She broke down all over again.

That night, not only did I lose my mother, but I also lost my father.

I was so confused and had no idea about what to do next. But I knew one thing. I knew that I could not go back home. And I didn't want to be alone so I called Chance.

By then, it was almost three o'clock in the morning. But I didn't know who else to call. I didn't even think to call Vartan. He was actually the last person on my mind.

So, I asked Chance to come and pick me up from the hospital. He was there in twenty minutes; he pulled up in a wet, candy colored BMW745. I had never seen his car, so I had no idea that he was rollin' like that!

I hugged Pleasure and told her that I needed some time to think and I'd call her in a day or so. Then I jumped in to the car with Chance and we pulled away.

"I'm sorry, Angell" Chance said as we rolled down Biscayne.

"Yeah me too" I said leaning back in the soft heated leather seat as we sat at the red light near the end of Biscayne.

Just then out of nowhere three thugs wearing ski masks surrounded the car. They were each armed with semi-automatic glocks.

"Get the fuck out the car! Get the fuck out now, nigga! And hurry up!" The second thug shouted as he stood beside the driver's side door and pressed his pistol against Chance's forehead.

"Fuck that! Just shoot that muthafucka! Then we can have some fun wit' his bitch!" The second thug said as he stood next to my door.

"Yeah, I'm finna smoke yo' ass!" The third masked carjacker said to Chance. Chance sat motionless, as the thug aimed his gun at Chance's temple. I screamed. And then the third masked man shouted.

"Wait! Wait!", as he ran around to the side of the car where Chance sat and looked at him closely. He paused.

Wait for what, nigga? We finna jack this mutha'fucka" The first thug said again.

The third guy whispered something into the ear of the first. And then...

"God was wit' chu' tonite! You musta been sayin' yo' prayers nigga"

The first thug said as he motioned to the other two and they all three ran off into the night. Disappearing just as fast as they came.

I sat trembling in my seat. I couldn't say a word. Chance was also quiet, but only in a different way. His quiet was calm, and undisturbed by what had just happened.

"Are you Okay?" Chance asked, looking at me as he touched my hand.

"Yeah, I think so", I responded.

"Good, let's get out of here" Chance said as he calmly drove away.

"Chance those niggas were gon' kill us! And you act like you ain't the least bit shaken up by that! Are you alright?" I asked, out of concern for his strangely steady and emotionless state.

"They weren't gonna kill us. They only wanted to scare us. They were just kids", Chance responded, as we got to I95 and made our way onto I-395. And then his phone rang, he looked at the caller I.D. display and answered. "Hello", he said. The person on the other began to speak and continued to talk for almost to minutes, but Chance never responded, except to say, "Okay, thanks", and then he shut the phone.

"Are you okay?" I asked.

"I'm fine." Chance responded, but in a way that let me know that he didn't want to be questioned. So, I left it alone.

"Where do you live again?' I asked wondering why we would be headed to this part of Miami.

"Not too far away, we're almost there!' He responded as he approached Hibiscus Island, one of the nicer areas of town.

Chance pulled up to the carport of a beautiful ocean side beach house, made of gorgeous peach colored sandstone.

"Well, this is it!" He said as he got out and looked at me. I got out and shut the door. We walked around to the back of the house, up the beautiful wooden steps.

It was chilly out; the crisp, clean air was blowing off the ocean. We quickly made our way up the stairs, to the sliding glass door and into the house, where we stood right in the center of the kitchen. It was dark, so Chance cut on the lights. He had a beautiful gourmet kitchen that was very neatly arranged.

"Follow me", he said.

We walked into the spacious living room. There was an earthy feel to the space that was decorated in 19th century Chinese décor. A clean smell of eucalyptus and citrus fruit filled the air.

We sat down on the huge comfortable sofa. I put my face into my hands. Chance looked at me quietly, for a moment.

"I can't believe she's gone! I mean, I know she was sick, but I thought we had just a little more time, ya' know?" I said as Chance sat back and looked up at the ceiling.

"Yeah, sometimes it feels like we have forever, but time makes fools of us all... Sit here, I'll go upstairs and make up your room. I wont be long. Help yourself to anything you want" Chance said as he got up from the couch and went upstairs. I looked around at the beautiful Asian art, it took me away for a moment.

My thoughts were stuck on my mother, and that dirty scoundrel who called himself her husband and my father. My heart was broken. Thoughts began to run wildly through my head.

"Was my father always a cheater?" I wondered. Maybe that was the reason for their nonexistent sexual relation. And maybe that was why he wasn't really pressed about sex, because he was getting plenty of it, just not from his wife.

My mother was a good woman. She didn't deserve to be disrespected like that. And if her nurse had been paying more attention to her, instead of concentrating on fucking my father, maybe my mother would still be alive. But at least her suffering was over.

I know it may sound strange, but it was almost a relief. Watching her die, I also died a little each day. Maybe if I had been there like I was supposed to, instead of be out trying to have a good time with Pleasure's hot ass, my mother might have still been alive, or maybe not.

The sound Of Chance's footsteps coming back down the stairs startled me. For a moment I actually forgot where I was. It's amazing how your thoughts can carry you away. And what's even more amazing is how reality can snatch you right back just as quickly,

"Everything's ready. I put new sheets on the bed, so they might feel a little scratchy, because they're right out of the pack. I just bought 'em. They're Egyptian cotton, Nordstrom's had a sale. So, um… anyway. You can go up anytime you get ready" Chance rambled nervously as he fidgeted and sat down in the chair next to the sofa where I was.

"Chance, I'm sorry for botherin' you like this. I just didn't know who else to call." I said as tears rolled down my face.

"What about Vartan? I mean… I'm sure he's probably worried about you. Don't you think you ought to at least let him know you're alright?" Chance responded.

"Vartan doesn't know yet, at least not from me anyway. We haven't talked in almost three days. I don't hear from him that much when he's on the road" I explained wiping my eyes with a tissue.

"He's probably just been busy. You should call him." Chance said politely.

"I don't wanna call him or anybody else right now! At this moment, all I wanna do is take a hot shower and lay down" I said as I exhaled in exhaustion.

"Come on. I'll show you where everything is" Chance said as he stood up and took my hand as walked upstairs to the masterbath.

"I'll set the shower for you. It's kind of tricky the first time." Chance said as he reached to adjust the water. It was beautiful! He had hibiscus flowers hanging everywhere and there were two small palm trees in each corner. It was like a lush tropical escape.

"Now, do you want all six shower heads turned on or just one?" Chance asked as the bathroom began to steam up like a private hibiscus jungle.

"I've never been inside a shower with six jets before. I am exhausted, I could use all six of 'em too." I said as I reached around & messaged the back of my stiff neck.

"There are fresh towels and terry cloth robes in the linen closet" (Chance Paused awkwardly) "Well, I'm sure that you can handle the rest from here. I'll be in the next room if you need anything else" Chance said as he smiled, walked out and shut the door.

After my shower I went to the guestroom and sat down on the bed by the window that faced out toward the beach.

I stopped and squinted my eyes, because I wasn't for sure but I thought I saw someone standing out by the shore. It looked like the same guy that I had seen earlier that night at the restaurant and before standing across the street from the school. My eyes came into to focus and I knew it was him, it had to be.

He seemed to be just standing there watching, as if he could see me through the dark from where he stood. I was almost in a trans. But just then, Chance walked in to the room and just about startled me to death. I screamed out loud.

"Oh my God! You scared me out of my wits! I didn't hear you come in" I said nervously.

"I'm sorry. I just came to see if you needed anything. Are you okay? You're shaking. Are you cold? Do you want me to turn the heat up?" Chance asked.

"Chance! Look! Look outside! There's a man standing on the beach. I saw him earlier tonight at the restaurant, and just before that across the street from the school. He's been following me all night and I think I saw him outside the hospital too, but I'm not sure" I whispered as if the guy on the beach could hear me from where he stood. Chance quickly stepped over next to the window and looked back at me.

"Angell, there's nobody out there. Are you sure you saw somebody?" Chance asked as his eyes surveyed the full stretch of the beach. But there was no one there. It was as if whoever it was had just vanished again.

At that point, I was pretty shaken up about my mother. I thought that maybe I could be just over reacting. So, I decided to try and put everything out of my mind and get some rest.

"I'll be in the next room if you need me" Chance said as he leaned down and kissed me on my forehead. I stared up at the ceiling and held my mother's face in my mind as I drifted of to sleep.

CHAPTER 12

When I woke up the next morning Chance was already downstairs fixing breakfast. He had the whole house smelling good. He was cooking steak with eggs and cheese, fresh homemade waffles and this delicious rose petal tea he bought from Hong Kong. He was talking on his cell phone, but abruptly ended his call when I entered the kitchen. "I'll have to talk to you about that later, goodbye." He said to who ever he was speaking to.

"I'm sorry. I didn't mean to interrupt. I just heard you downstairs and I ..." I fumbled for something to say.

"How did you sleep?" Chance asked as he smiled, politely evading my comment as he handed me a small Chinese teacup.

"Okay I guess" I responded. Still worn out and slight dazed from the night before.

I watched Chance as he moved about the gourmet kitchen, preparing our breakfast. He was wearing a white wife beater and a pair of grey sweats. It was hardly the way that I was use to seeing him dressed but he was still hella-sexy.

Chance and I sat outside on the kitchen deck and ate. The food was wonderful but I didn't have much of an appetite. All I could do is think of my mother. Chance didn't say much. He didn't need to. Just being near him was all I needed at that moment.

In the short time that we had known each other, we had actually become quite close. Through our lunchtime talks and the walks from our classrooms at night after school, I had come to know Chance quite well.

It's funny how your feelings for a person can grow out of nowhere. Sometimes I would be alone at home or in my car just driving and Chance would always manage to find his way into my thoughts. I never imagined that one day I would be sitting across from him, at his house, having breakfast, after spending the night in his bed.

Chance's presence was calming. I found myself being carried away by the sound of his deep, full voice and getting lost in the soulfulness of his eyes.

When I was near him, for moments at a time I was his prisoner and he never even knew it.

I was almost in a paradise that couldn't be disturbed, until Chance's phone rang. It was Mrs. Tillman, the vice principal form Miramar High School. She said that she was calling to send her condolences and to see if I was okay, because I had called her earlier and left a message about my mother's passing. I told her that I would need a few days off to handle things, and that I could be reached at Chance's house if she needed me. I had turned my cell Phone off the night before, because I wasn't in any shape to talk to anybody, especially my father.

Mrs. Tillman also said that I had like fifteen messages from Vartan. He had been calling all over the school looking for me, asking the other teachers if they had heard from me and he was also asking about Chance. Apparently, Pleasure had called him the night before to tell him about my mother's death, and in that same conversation she must have also told him that Chance had come to get me from the hospital.

So, I figured that I would call Vartan and let him know that I was okay, just in case he really did care. He was usually so busy with his team and his fans that sometimes it was hard to tell where his head was.

Chance began to clear the dishes from outside and I went upstairs to get my phone and call Vartan. When I cut it on I had twenty-four voice messages waiting and elevens text messages, most of them from Vartan and Pleasure. And there was also a couple from my father.

I dialed Vartan's number several times but there was no answer. Then the next time I tried to call, it just went straight to voicemail. I finally just left a text saying that I was okay and that I would try to call again later.

Since Chance had asked me to stay with him until I got my head together, I needed to go shopping for a few things, because I had left home in such rush and didn't have any clothes and stuff with me. So we got ready and headed out to the mall near Ball harbor. I was really torn up but I figured it would do me some good to get out and get some fresh air. And just as we got into the car to leave, my cell phone rang. It was an unknown number. I answered it out of reflex.

"Hello" I said hesitantly, thinking that it was probably my father.

"Yeah! I'm only gonna warn you once. Stay the fuck away from my man. He's finished wit 'cho high siditty, fake, wannabe Virgin Mary ass! We finna have another baby. So, leave us alone and don't let me have to tell yo' ass again!" An angry female voice shouted from the other end and hung up before I could even get a word in edge wise.

When we were getting ready to leave the mall, Chance said he'd bring it around to the front. So I stood by the revolving door with my bags. There were some kids laughing and running around by the escalators, and one of them tripped and fell, and his fingers had gotten caught in the grids of the escalator stairs and pulled him in, twisting and mangling his hand into a bloody stump. It was horrible.

But what I saw next after that tragic site was even more frightening. There next to the escalator, in the midst of all the panic and commotion was the guy in the hooded sweatshirt. The same little light skinned guy that I had seen the night before, at the restaurant and again at the hospital.

It was him, and even with all the panic and screaming that was going on right in front of him; his eyes were locked on me. It was almost like he was in some kind of trace. And then Chance pulled up to the front of the mall and blew his horn. I turned to look out at Chance and when I turned back around the guy in the hoodie was gone. He had disappeared again just like the time before.

I turned on my cell phone to call Chance, but panic took over and I ran though the revolving door, almost knocking down a lady and her three small kids. I hurried to the car, yanking the door open and scurrying inside. Chance looked at me like I was crazy.

"Did you see him? He was in there! He stood right next to the boy that got his hand caught in the escalator! There was blood everywhere, but he acted like he didn't even notice it. He just kept staring at me! This nigga is stalkin' me!" I shouted looking back at the mall doors.

"Who? Angell, who are you talking about?"

Chance responded looking all around us.

"The guy in the grey sweat shirt! It was the same guy I saw three times last night by the school and at the restaurant, and again outside your house on the beach" I shouted hysterically.

"Well, where is he now?" Chance asked as he started to get out of the car to run back inside the mall.

"No, he's gone. He disappeared again, just like before. I know you are starting to think that I'm crazy, but there is somebody following me! I know it is!" I shouted.

I got inside the car and Chance pulled away. He took me back to his house and put on a pot of tea to help settle my nerves. We sat out on the deck and watched the sunrise set over the ocean.

"This is some place you have, Chance! Four bedrooms, three baths, a gourmet kitchen, two fireplaces, a sunken hot tub and a beach view! The rent must be unbelievable! How do afford something like this?" I commented as we sipped our tea.

"There's no rent. This property belongs to me" Chance replied as he looked out at the beach as two people walked by holding hands.

"You own this house? How do you afford to live like this? I don't know any other art teachers that are rolling a brand new 745 and Range Rover and own a beach house" I remarked curiously.

"You would be surprised what you could do if you budget. And my Beamer is not brand new, its two years old." Chance said as he smiled facetiously, got up from his seat and walked over to the wood railing of the deck.

Though Chance answered my questions freely, I could tell that he was a bit uncomfortable. I was just curious to know how an art teacher could afford a lifestyle like this on such a modest salary! But I decided to drop it for the time being.

Chance stood looking out at the tide without saying a word, with his back turned to me. The light from the setting sun bounced off his long muscular arms, and his broad shoulders filled the recesses of his G-unit wife beater.

I got up from my chair, walked over and stood beside Chance on the deck. He glanced at me slightly. The tats on his arms caught my eye. They said something in Chinese. I touched his skin with my fingertip, gently tracing along the outline of his tattoos.

Chance continued to watch the surf break softly against the shoreline. The muscles in his arms flexed on their own as I took both of my hands and firm squeezed his large biceps.

I had imagined touching him this way so many times. Some nights I would fall asleep in my bed thinking about him so hard that my thoughts would turn into dreams. But tonight I was actually standing next to him, touching him, caressing him! Though I was wide-awake, I knew my dreams were coming true.

Chance turned around and looked into my eyes. His stare was hypnotic. I shivered as a slight breeze brushed against my skin. Chance ran his hands along my arms to warm me.

He leaned into me and nestled his cheek against mine. I caressed his face, as our lips met and brushed against each other. Time seemed to stand still.

I closed my eyes in anticipation of his kiss. Chance wrapped his arms around me and held me close with his lips just millimeters away from mine. And then...

My cell phone began to ring. I must have forgotten to cut it back off earlier after all the commotion at the mall. It was Pleasure. I could tell by the distinctive ring tone. Playing Keyshia Cole's "Let Him Go".

It stopped ringing. Chance touched me and once more our eyes locked. But then, phone started ringing again. I wasn't going to answer it, but she kept calling back to back to back. Chance stepped slightly to the side. I walked over into the kitchen by the door and grabbed my purse.

"What up girl" I answered breathing deeply.

"Are you someplace where you can talk?" Pleasure asked with a peculiar tone to her voice.

"Pleasure, I am really not in the mood to talk right now! Tell my father I will see him at the funeral. I don't have anything to say, especially to him" I responded curtly.

"Well, girl I think you're gonna want to listen to what I have to say. It's about Vartan" She replied.

"Look I already told you... I don't wanna hear it!" I replied.

"If you're near a T.V. you'll wanna turn to ESPN or FOX NEWS. They're talking about 'cho boy" Pleasure insisted.

"I don't wanna hear about his touchdowns, his field-goals or his fumbles, none of that shit! My mother just died and I just can't..." I asserted as Pleasure abruptly cut me off.

"Angell, Vartan is in jail! He was arrested this afternoon in Cincinnati! It's been all over the news. I'm surprised you haven't already heard" Pleasure said as her voice softened.

"What? Arrested for what? Another D.U.I. charge?" I asked nonchalantly.

"He's been arrested for 1st degree murder", she said.

"Why are you trippin?" I asked.

I'm not trippin'. It's true Angell! They found a girl shot to death in his hotel room." She struggled to speak.

"A girl? What girl? Who was she?" I asked as I felt a knot tighten in the pit of my stomach, suspecting that I already knew what Pleasure's reply would be.

"It was Dilonda Lovetts! Pleasure said as her voice weakened and my suspicion was realized.

"Dilonda Lovett? What was Vartan doing with that nasty ass project bitch?" I said as tears welled up in my eyes. Chance looked on helplessly at my distress.

"The news didn't say! And I've been trying to call this guy that I know, who plays on the team with Vartan. But he's not answering the phone. I'm gonna keep trying though. I promise!" Pleasure said as I walked into the living room and cut on the T.V. The station was already on FOX News.

"Details are still sketchy, but what is known right now is that Vartan Daniels, quarterback for the Miami Maxx was arrested in Cincinnati,

Ohio this afternoon in connection with a brutal homicide.

Apparently, a woman was found dead, the victim of several gunshot wounds. She has been identified as twenty-six year old, Dilonda Lovetts, of Liberty City, Florida. It is still not clear what the victim's relationship was to the quarterback of the Miami-Maxx. Vartan Daniel was lead away in handcuffs and declined comment as he passed by the media. He is being held tonite without bond in the Hamilton County Justice Center"

I dropped the phone and collapsed to my knees in front of the television set. Chance ran over and knelt down beside me. I fell into his arms and cried like a baby.

"First my mother, then my no good ass father, and now, this! What's next? Chance, I can't take no more!" I sobbed, as everything around me seemed to come apart.

Chance turned off the television set, and sat me down, spouting tears like a water fountain.

The pain inside my heart was greater than anything I could have ever imagined. It was more intense than any hurt I had ever known. At that moment Chance was my only comfort.

"All my life I have been told that as long as I trusted and believed in God, everything would be alright. My mother said that Jesus would never see the righteous forsaken. But look at me.

I spent my whole life trying to do what was right. I was always obedient; I always tried to be honest and respectable. I said my prayers and read my bible everyday. Hell, I even looked both ways before I cross the damn street.

I saved myself for one man, and now God has taken that away too. All this time, I've been keeping myself pure and for what? Maybe there is no right or wrong. I would even say that maybe there is no God, but I know better. I've felt his love and seen his power too many times. (I paused) Chance, why can't I feel him now? Where is he now? Where is God?" I cried, soaking the pillow with my tears as Chance sat quietly beside me.

"Chance, I've never heard you mention God. Do you believe in God?" I asked lifting my head up from the pillow.

"I believe in God! I know that God is real. I know that he is, because I see him everyday. I see him in the eyes of small children who have never seen evil. I see him in the faces of the hungry and the poor. I see him in the tears of the broken hearted. I saw him inside of you the first time we met" Chance said as he touched my cheek with the back of his hand.

"My mother dedicated herself to God, to her husband and to the church. And I always swore to do the same thing, but now I don't know." I said with uncertainty.

"Of all the places where I have seen God's love and kindness, the church is where I've seen it the least. People congregate every week, put on their fancy clothes and drive their fancy cars, only to impress each other, because none of that is impressive to God. They walk right by the poor and broken hearted, on the way into their big, beautiful church buildings that are all trimmed in gold, but they leave the spirit of God outside.

I'm sorry! As you can probably tell, I'm not a huge fan of the church!" Chance said as he stood by the window with his eyes still watching the surf. "Well, it's been a long day. You should try to get some rest. I'll be right next door if you need me".

Chance said as he walked toward the doorway.

"Chance wait! I don't wanna be by myself. Will you stay with me again tonight, please" I asked as I sat up in bed.

"Angell, I don't know if that's such a good idea! Chance replied at just above a whisper as he looked down at the Japanese hardwood floor.

"Chance, please stay with me tonight!" I begged as I got up from the bed, walked over to Chance and took hold of his hands. We stood at the doorway and looked into each other's eyes. I lead Chance back inside and over to the bed. I laid down and faced the window. Chance sat down on the bed and ran his fingers through my short, dark, wavy hair. His touch soothed the turmoil inside my soul. I pulled Chance toward me, nestled myself inside his arms and I closed my eyes to rest.

CHAPTER 13

When I woke up it was early morning just before dawn, I felt so safe with Chance wrapped around me, as though nothing else in the world could get through.

I laid in Chance's arms all night. He hid me deep within the strength of his fortress where I could have stayed forever. Chance welcomed me with open arms into his home. Even with all my drama, he shared his peace with me.

Truthfully, I had been feeling him all along, from the very first day that we met in the teacher's lounge. I kept telling myself that he was just another co-worker, just another teacher I spent time with during lunch and planning periods. But nothing was farther from the truth. I knew from that first hello, from that first smile that this was bound to be much more than just something casual.

When laid inside his arms that night, I knew it was love. Even though I belonged to someone else. Once I met Chance it was pretty much over for Vartan. Meeting him actually made me ask myself if what I had with Vartan was really love at all. Or was I just settling? Settling for some rich, handsome, conceited, arrogant, hard headed son of a bitch that had developed a strong taste for money, cars and ho's.

Chance stole my heart because he was nothing at all like Vartan. He was quiet, but his strength filled the room. He was humble, what he did was from his heart and not for show. And he was so down to earth, I mean, I would have never known that he had money just by talking to him. Because he never flashed or flossed what he had.

However, I must admit that I was really curious to know how Chance was able to afford the luxury cars, the beach house and all that expensive Asian art.

And there was one other thing that I was dying to know. Who was the girl in the pictures all over his dresser? I wasn't trying to be nosy but I peeked my head in yesterday, just to see what was in there. And I saw some pictures of this girl. She was a cute light skinned girl, and as dark as he was I knew that she couldn't have been his sister. But there were like fifty photos of her, so she must have been somebody important.

But he said that he didn't have a girlfriend, so who was she?

I thought to myself as I held him close and watched the sun come up over the ocean.

Last night was amazing. I felt really comfortable laying there next to Chance, but I had to go to the bathroom and pee real bad. So I eased up slowly from the bed. Chance turned over on to his other side, and I hurried into restroom to relieve my bladder, and take a quick shower. As I was coming from the bathroom, I heard my cell phone ringing, so, I went downstairs to get it. I flipped the phone open and answered.

"Hello" I said, clearing my voice.

"Hey Angell. I just called to see how you were. I never heard back from you last night and I called you back like twenty times, but I guess you were busy. Are you okay?" Pleasure asked.

"I'm doing Okay, I guess." I responded still half asleep.

"I just wanted let you know that your dad scheduled the funeral for next Saturday morning at eleven. It's going to be at the church of course. So, he wanted us all to leave here in the limo together about ten o'clock." She said, then pausing to wait on my response, but I had none.

"You are coming home to go to the funeral with us, right?" Pleasure asked, and again she waited on my response, there was none.

"Come on, Angell! Don't do this to your Dad, he's going through a lot as it is! Pleasure said.

"He's going through a lot as it is? Fuck that! I don't give a damn about what he's going through! Fuck him and fuck you too! You stay, so far up his ass, that you can probably taste what he just swallowed! And you know what else? You were always with him, so you probably knew what the hell he had been up to all along. Did you know that he was cheatin' on my mother? Did you know, Pleasure? Tell me the truth!" I shouted into the phone.

"What? NO! I didn't know anything! I swear!" she responded.

"Yes you did! That's why you pushed me into going out for dinner and drinks. You were the decoy to keep me out of the house until he could get his nut off. You foul ass bitch! I knew you were scandalous the first time I met you!

You are such a stank ho and you been a ho' since we were kids. And yo' tramp ass was the reason your grandma's house got blown up. Because you were out being hot and flirting wit' them dope boys that day before church. Your grandma came outside to get you and she called the police on Boom-Boom, that was the night he set yo' house on fire. You stupid bitch, you're fuckin' the nigga that killed yo' granny!"

Pleasure held the phone silently, which made me even madder, so I tore into her ass some more.

"Bitch! Don't act like you didn't know that it was you who got yo' grandma killed, messin wit' that dope boy. You just a nasty church ho! And since you love my damn daddy so much, y'all can have each other!

Oh, and before I go, tell me something. I've been dying to know how you can get up every Sunday and sing songs about purity and holiness, and still be the biggest freak in Miami?

And to think that I kept all of your dirty little secrets, about your thug lover, yo' STD's, the abortion you had! I knew everything but I never told a soul! How do you look at yo' self in the mirror?" I shouted into the phone as the other end went dead. Pleasure hung up and I still felt like shit. I thought that yelling at her would make me feel better, but it didn't. I felt just as lousy as I did before.

Chance stood at the top of the stairs listening to me. Then he slowly walked down and stood two steps from the bottom, shocked, eyeing me as if he didn't want to look at me.

"Was that your sister that you were just talking to on the phone?" Chance asked as he stepped all the way down into the living room.

"Yeah, I guess so!" I replied

"Wow, if that's how you talk to people you love, I'd hate to hear what you'd say to somebody you hate!" he commented as he moved into the kitchen to start breakfast.

"What was that all about? He inquired.

"It's complicated. I wouldn't even know where to start!" I responded, trailing behind him into the kitchen.

"You like granola? I've got some fruit in here too. Or we could just go out and grab something. It's a real nice breakfast spot over on South Beach." Chance said as he looked into the empty fridge.

"Okay, but I gotta make a quick call first!" I said as I walked back into the living room to get my cell phone and began to dial, but before I could finish, the phone rang again. It was a strange number, a 513 area code.

"Hello!" I answered curiously.

"Baby, it me! Listen, I only have five minutes! Theses mutha'fuckas in here are trippin'", a man shouted.

"Vartan? Is that you? What's gong on? What happened?" I asked anxiously.

"I did it for us, baby! I had to! That bitch was talkin' about going to the media and holding press conferences and shit! I had to shut that bitch up!" Vartan said as he starting rattling off on the phone.

"Vartan, No! Don't tell me that what they're sayin' is true! No! You did not kill Dilonda Lovetts. Tell me you didn't, please, Vartan!" I begged in disbelief.

I'm sorry, baby! I had to! She was finna mess up everything. I tried to give her some money to have an abortion but she wouldn't. I was already giving the bitch $10,000 a month for my other son! He rattled off, as the hair on the back of my neck stood up

"Vartan, What did you just say? What other son? You got a baby? Don't tell me you done had a kid since we was in high school and you're just now telling me!" So, how old is this child? Seven or eight. Vartan?" I asked as my heart began to pound.

"He's a year old, Angell" Vartan said solemnly as the blood rushed to my head and the room began to spin.

"No wonder that bitch was always at every game and always hanging around! But you told me that Rondell Wexler was fuckin her!" I shouted into the phone.

"He was. I mean, we both were, but when the paternity test came back, it said that I was the baby's daddy!" Vartan continued.

"Baby?" I again shouted in shock, trying to interject.

"So I started giving her money so she wouldn't go public and so that she wouldn't tell you.

"But then she called last week and told me that she was pregnant again!" he said as I almost fainted.

"Pregnant again?" I asked as my hands tremble, now barely able to hold the phone.

"Yeah, but this time she had a lawyer. She said that he figured that I should be paying her like $19,000 a month plus back pay for the other baby. So, I told her to fly up and meet me in Cincinnati so we could talk about it. I went and got a motel room after the game. She waited on me to check in.

When I got there, she just started going off, talking about how she was finna really get paid and how she was gonna tell you everything, and then I just snapped. I pulled out the gun that I carried for protection and shot her. Then I had to make sure that if she really was pregnant and that the baby didn't survive. So I shot her twice in the stomach. I did it for us! I did this shit for us!" Vartan yelled through the phone. I began to shake all over.

"Look baby! I gotta go! But I just want you to know that I love you and I'll be outta here in no time. They can't keep me in here, I gotz too much money. I got over 45 million dollars in the bank and I want you to be my wife and have my babies. Y'all wont ever want for anything. I swear!" Vartan said.

I paused to regroup.

"Vartan. I don't know what to say, except... You must have lost yo' mutha' fuckin mind! I don't want anything else to do with you. You killed your own child! I don't want to talk to you! I don't want your money! And I damn 'sho don't wanna be your wife! I trusted you and you lied, about everything! It's over Vartan! We are through! So, don't chu' ever call me again! I'll see you on the news. Goodbye!" I said as I shut the phone and cried out loud in agony. I ran into the kitchen sobbing and through myself into Chance's arms. Chance consoled me without a word.

I was in total despair. The next few days just sort of went by in a blur. I spent most of my time walking the beach, replaying each moment of my life that lead me to this point.

I thought about my childhood and how I grew up. I remembered watching everybody come to church all dressed up in their Sunday's best. Everybody was looking good, smelling good, and putting their last dollars and dimes into the collection plate, even though they were barely able to pay their rent and put food on the table.

Being the daughter of a high profile church pastor allowed me many opportunities to see things from the inside that most people would never see.

I saw the two faced preachers that sat in the pulpit and preached the word. They warned everybody else to be holy and to fear the wrath of God, while they themselves took part in every type of lying, cheating, stealing and freakin' that they could manage to think of.

Take Pastor Tendley for instance, who led a yearly revival and protest against gays and the homosexual agenda. Why was he was caught at a gay strip club in downtown Miami by the police during a prostitution sting? The pastor said that he was only there to pray for the gay men and lead them to Christ. Maybe that's why the police found him bent over on his knees screaming for Jesus.

Then there was Bishop Ketts, he went to jail for stealing from the church's building fund. This dumb ass nigga was taking $2500 a month to pay for the new house that he had built in Broward County. He must have been confused about which building the "church's building fund" was supposed to be funding.

Then there was Elder Whittendale, who had eight kids and four baby-mama's, and they all attended his church. Every Sunday there would be some kind of drama, because he was remarried for the second time, but still messin' around with both his ex-wives and his youngest child's mother. It was some absolute craziness. But that's the type of foolishness you were likely to find in the church on any given Sunday.

As I looked back on it all, church folks were some of the funniest characters that I had ever met, and some of the saddest. See, at least with street people or "worldly folks", as church folks called them, you pretty much knew what you were getting.

If a guy was a player, you pretty much knew it by the way that he approached you and the lines that he used in order to get a woman's attention. There was really no way to miss it.

If a girl was a ho' or a gold digger, you could pretty much tell by the way she dressed, the way she walked, and what she had to say when she spoke. I mean, some ho's try to be under cover, but for the most part, they pretty much represent at face value, as do most people on the street.

It's like this, a pimp is a pimp, a player is a player, and a hustler is a hustler, and most of them can be spotted from a mile away. But most church folks wear at least two faces. One face is for the other church folks, one face is for the folks they're perpetratin' for on the streets (pretending like that they're holy, when they're really more full of the devil than Satan himself).

And there's the face that they only reveal at home (the real Brother So and So, the real Sister Such and Such). This is the face they put on when they cuss, clown, and abuse their families. It's the face they show when they are drunk as a skunk and higher than a kite.

And then there's the final and most honest face. This is the most terrifying face of all; it's the face they show when nobody is around. This is the face that nobody sees but God and the man in the mirror. This is the face that knows their private thoughts and knows every secret sin of the heart.

I spent my entire life believing in something that never existed, watching men exalting themselves and fatten their pockets, while they overlooked the needs of the poor. Most of today's churches are no more than glorified fashion shows, gossip pits and dating games. I never thought I would see the day when you could get 'cho holla on in a church easier than you could at the club. But maybe it's always been that way and I just needed to grow up before I could understand the truth.

Whatever the case, one thing was for sure. I was sick and tired of all the nonsense and hypocrisy that I saw around me. And I didn't want anything else to do with it. I wasn't turning my back on God, just the three-ring circus that masqueraded itself as his church.

I was so scared, because for the first time in my life I was alone and I had no one to depend on besides God. I had always had my mother and father to lean on; they were always right there. My mother told me that she would always be around if I ever needed her. If she only knew how badly I needed her now.

Me and my father were close too, in a strange way. Even though he was always busy doing something with the church, I felt like he was always there, though most of the time he really wasn't. His body was at home with us, but his mind was usually at least ten other places.

But he was doing the work of the Lord, building God's church, and hustlin' God's children.

The more I thought about it, the more that I started to see the whole thing for what it really was, it was a scam, a con game, a bait and switch.

They had taken something sacred and turned it into a sideshow, complete with dancing clowns and snake oil salesmen. The whole thing was nothing more than a staged routine set up to bilk the crowd out of their money. They called themselves missionaries, but the true meaning of the mission had been lost.

Where was I gonna go now? The church was all that I knew. They were my family and my friends. And since I had seen life for what it truly was, I had lost everything. At least that's the way it felt.

Imagine waking up one day to find out that everything you had been taught was a lie, and everything that you believed was a complete and total scam! You looked in the mirror and found out that you had been walking around with the word "Sucker" tatted on your forehead. If you can imagine that, then you can imagine how I felt at that very moment.

"When I imagine the size of the universe, and I wonder what's out past the edges. I've discovered inside me a space as big, and believe that I'm meant to be filled up with more than just questions", songwriter, Chris Rice.

CHAPTER 14

It was the morning before my mother's funeral. The sunrise was covered by thick clouds and the air was heavy and humid. The atmosphere rumbled with the threat of severe storms. I was surrounded by an uneasiness that I had never felt before.

I looked over at Chance as he slept. Inside his arms was the only place I found rest. He held me close without any expectation. His affection for me was completely unselfish. His touch was a gift meant only to calm the turmoil that brewed within me. He asked for nothing, but he gave me everything.

He had made himself the guardian of my heart, in his care I was untouchable. I had lost everything, but he gave me his peace, a peace I could not understand. And for this kindness I was grateful beyond words. Chance had become my heart's protection and my mind's refuge.

I hated the mornings, because the morning sounded for me to be released from his embrace. The morning demanded that I walk alone. I was left to confront all my thoughts and fears on my own in the daylight.

That morning I looked outside the window at the beach. It seemed to be calling out to me, offering me peace if I would just walk along it's sands. So, I quietly got up from the bed, made my way to the bathroom, took a shower and stuff. Then I made my way downstairs and out of the kitchen door to the beach.

My toes meshed into the sand. The smell of the sea breeze got stronger as I got closer to the shore. The sound of the tide relaxed me as I began to walk.

Tomorrow was my mother's funeral. This was the day that she and I would say our last goodbye. It was more than twenty-four hours away, but it seemed like only twenty-four seconds.

I could feel the anxiety building as I headed up the beach. I couldn't believe my mother was gone. The night before, I almost picked up the phone to call and tell her about Vartan. I actually dialed half the number before I realized that she wasn't even there anymore.

I began to pray and talk to God. I wanted to know why things had turned out the way they did in my life. I wanted to know why and how it was possible for me to have done everything he said do, but yet be left with absolutely nothing.

I wanted to know why he let me live a lie for so many years? How could the people that claimed to care so much mislead me? I wanted to know how my mother could be such a good woman, a woman that did so much for others, and did so little for herself, a woman who trusted in him for everything, how could she end up used and made a fool of?

I even asked why I had to be made dark skinned and boney. I had a shape but most men (black men) preferred thicker women. Why couldn't I be light skinned with pretty eyes and a body like WHOA?

I had walked about a mile just as it began to sprinkle. I kept going for almost another half mile before I decided to turn around as the rumble of thunder grew closer. The gray in the sky deepened and the droplets of water got bigger and more frequent.

My leisurely walk turned into a light jog as the storm moved closer and the sky darkened.

A fierce wind swept across the beach in the opposite direction that I was headed. A flash of lightning struck in the distance over the ocean. I began to quicken my pace.

Just then, off to the side of the beach, someone was standing by the road that led from the shore. I couldn't make out who it was. But who ever it was, they were just standing there in the rain.

I was just about halfway back to the house, but I was out of breath. I had to stop and rest. The person by the side of the road was still standing there. They were wearing and hooded raincoat. I couldn't see their face.

I became uncomfortable. I couldn't tell if they were just standing there minding their own business or if they were watching me.

I pulled myself together and got back on my jog. I only had a little further to go, but the rain was starting to come down harder. The person standing off to the side of the road remained in place as I passed. I tried not to look at him, but I couldn't help it.

And then, our eyes met, and the stranger took one step forward toward me. And I slowed down slightly, struggling to see through the rain.

It was the same guy that had been following me. I paused for a second in fear. But that same fear then caused me to run like hell!

I looked back to see where he was. He was in the middle of the beach, walking quickly in my direction. I began to scream for Chance as I approached to the house and ran up the steps from the beach.

I opened the sliding glass door to the kitchen and slammed it shut behind me. Chance came running down the stairs into the kitchen.

I told him that I had seen that guy again that he had been following me, and he was down on the beach and was coming this way. I was hysterical. I could barely talk.

Chance rushed out of the glass door, out in to the rain, down the steps and out on to the beach. I ran out on to the deck, and watched as Chance carefully surveyed the area, looking up and down the beach around the houses and even out into the surf. But the guy had disappeared again.

Chance stared up at me from the beach and then started to walk back up to the house. The rain was now coming down in buckets and Chance was soaked to skin. I stood at the door and tried to dry his face with a clean towel from the kitchen pantry.

He didn't say anything, but I knew that he was slightly frustrated by what he considered to be another false alarm. He took the towel and wiped his head. I stood at his glass door, looking outside, angry at myself for looking like a fool. But I was becoming more frightened now than embarrassed.

Chance walked up to the living room to make sure that he didn't see anyone outside from the front window. And of course, there was no one out there. Chance walked back into the kitchen and turned on his tea pot.

I walked over to him, stood in his face, and pulled his wet tank top over his head. It was soaking wet. I dropped it on the floor and looked at Chance in his eyes. I stepped in closer to him.

I felt a sudden rush as my heart began to pound. I moved even closer into his personal space and put my arms around him. My stomach began to tighten with nervous jitters.

I leaned my head against him and pressed my lips against his chest. His torso was hard and conditioned. His pecks flexed each time I kissed them.

He put his arms around me and slowly ran his hand down my shoulders to my arms and a long my hip. I had never given myself permission to touch a man this way and I sure as hell had never ever given any man the permission to me touch like this.

Chance's skin was a creamy dark coco that matched his eyes. He was more than sexy; this man had an unstoppable carnal magnetism that couldn't even be put into words. But I didn't need any words, because the time for talking was done.

Chance put his arms around me firmly and pressed his lips against my forehead. He breathed in deeply, smelling my hair and my skin, as he brushed his lips across my ear lobe and to my neck. I could feel the heat from his mouth as he began to gently kiss my shoulder.

An intense chill ran from the top of my head all the way to my toes as he touched my face and we again locked eyes, moving closer together.

CHAPTER 15

And then, like a cry in the night... that damn Chinese teapot whistled! It was loud as hell! It sounds like we were standing in the middle of a train yard.

I pulled away quickly regaining myself control. Chance turned around and cut the fire off the black tea kettle that was engraved with three golden Chinese characters.

The whistle seemed to scream stop. So I stopped. Chance remained facing toward the stove. And I moved back over to the glass door, looking out at the beach. And then Chance's phone began to ring.

Chance quickly walked over to the corner of the kitchen, looked at the caller I.D and snatched the phone from the cradle. He looked at me strangely, and abruptly excused himself. He told me he would be right back and went to talk downstairs in the garage.

That reminded me of my own telephone call that needed to be made. So, I went upstairs and pulled out my cell phone. I needed to call

Pleasure and apologize for some of the things I said to her the last time we talked.

I had actually had sometime to think and my conscience was really putting a whipping on me. I knew that I was just hurting and frustrated and I took my hurt out on her.

During my talk with God, while I was reminding him about my hurt and the short comings of everybody else. He quickly reminded me of my need to forgive those who had hurt me. That would include Pleasure as well as a couple of other folks. But I need to start with her. So, I dialed her number.

"Hello" Pleasure answered, sounding half asleep.

"Hey, girl, Are you busy?" I asked.

"No, I'm cool. What's up?" She replied in a somewhat dry tone.

"I wanted to apologize. Those were some pretty mean things I said to you the last time we talked and I just wanna say that I'm sorry. I had no right to come at you like that. And I hope you can forgive me." I said as silence claimed the phone line. And then, Pleasure busted into tears. She began sobbing so heavily that I couldn't even understand what she was saying.

"What? Hey, Pleasure! Pleasure! Are you okay?" I asked over and over again.

"You hurt me so bad! I never knew that you thought of me that way! I know that I have my faults and things I struggle with, but I'm trying. I never knew that you saw me as some dirty whore. I love you like a sister" She cried.

"I'm sorry, Pleasure. Please forgive me, girl! I never meant to hurt you. I love you, not like a sister, but as my sister." I said as I struggled to make things right.

I apologized and made peace with Pleasure, and I knew the next thing I had to do was to set things right with my father. But I was still so angry. I felt so betrayed by what he had done to my mother. She was a strong believer in God and she loved my father unconditionally. She sacrificed everything for her family. And on the last night of her life, her husband committed the worst act of treachery imaginable. She did not deserve that!

And why did I have to be the one to catch him in the act? Thinking about it made me sick! I wish had never known, but wishes only came true in fairytales. The reality was that I was stuck with some very deep wounds that might never heal.

After I hung up with Pleasure, I laid back and stretched out on the bed, I was exhausted both mentally and physically. But I had to find the strength somewhere to face what lay ahead tomorrow.

My eye-lids were heavy, they burned from lack of sleep. I had to rest my mind and get away from my thoughts for just a while. Sleep was calling to me. So, I decided to take a short nap.

It was eight o'clock at night. A loud lightning strike and a great roll of thunder awakened me. Apparently I had been asleep all afternoon and most of the evening.

I rolled over to cut on the lamp by the bed. The power was out due to the storm. I opened the bedroom door and walked out into the hallway to find Chance, but he wasn't in his room or in the bathroom. I called his name but there was no answer. So I felt along the wall and made my way downstairs.

When I reached the bottom of the steps there seemed to be a soft glowing light coming from the kitchen. There was Chance, he had the whole downstairs lit up with candles.

He was fixing dinner. He had ordered take out from Maxine's, this really great little soul food joint downtown.

"I thought you might be hungry", he said as he pulled out a tall bamboo stool for me to sit on at the counter.

Everything was set up so nice. He got us fried chicken, green beans, candied yams, and sweet cornbread. And there was fresh chilled fruit for dessert.

"You were in a coma up there, you must have been really tired" he said as he fixed our plates.

"Yeah I was pretty worn out. I guess I needed the rest. This looks really good. I'm starvin too." I said as my mouth watered looking at the delicious spread.

"I thought that maybe we could pick up where we left off earlier today." Chance said, smiling slightly to one side, showing his dimples as he poured two glasses of wine.

"Tomorrow's the funeral", I said, looking down at the plate of steaming food. The divine aroma hit my nose and aroused my pallet.

"Yeah, I know. And I'll be right there for you." Chance touched my hand.

"Well, we should bless the food before it gets cold." Chance said as he took hold of my hand and began to pray.

"Heavenly father, we thank you for this food and for always remembering us with your kindness. Please give us your strength to lean on and your wisdom to see us through. Bless you father, Amen."

I know that this is going to sound a little strange and I'm almost ashamed to admit it, but hearing Chance pray did something to me. Seeing this part of him actually sort of turned me on in a physical way. I had to shake myself and get a grip on my hormones.

"My mother gave her whole life to my father and he played her." I said as I thought out loud.

"Love is a risk. It's actually the greatest risk of all. Sometimes you win, other times you lose. But you can't win or lose if you never take the risk" Chance said as he stared outside at the rain.

"So, if somebody were to give their love to you, what would be the risk?" I asked as I touched the frost on the wine glass with my fingertip.

"What are you asking me?" Chance replied as he leaned forward on the counter and stared deeply into my eyes.

"I need to know, what is the risk of Chance?" I asked.

"The risk of Chance?" (He laughed) "You make me sound dangerous" he replied.

"Are you" I asked as I leaned forward and stared back at him with the same intensity, hoping to provoke his honest response.

"We're all in danger of one thing or another, whether we realize it or not." Chance replied as he stood up to clear our dinner plates.

After we ate, we sat in the sunroom and looked up at the sky as the storm passed. I was so relaxed that I had actually started to put everything out of my head for a moment. And then... my cell phone rang.

CHAPTER 16

It was a little after midnight. I glanced down at the phone knowing full well who it was by the ringtone. It was Pleasure. "What could she possibly want at this time of the night?" I said out loud.

"You should answer that, it could be important." Chance said as he handed me the phone from the coffee table.

"Hello" I answered.

"Angell, I'm in Overtown. Can you come get me? Please!" Pleasure said, she sounded as though she had been crying.

"Overtown? What's going on? And what are you doing in Overtown at this time of the night?" I asked, struggling to hear her over the background of where ever she was calling from. It sounded like a party was going on behind her, but she didn't sound too festive.

"Please Angell! Just come and get me! I'll explain everything when you get here!" Pleasure cried into the phone.

"Okay! Okay! But I don't have my car" I said.

"Take my car!" Chance said as he stood up and walked into the kitchen to get the keys to his BMW.

Pleasure gave me the address to where she was. Chance wanted to go with me but Pleasure insisted that I come alone, in fact she made me promise.

So, he hesitantly let me go and I flew through downtown to get Pleasure. I followed the directions she gave me. She was at this house around the corner from the neighborhood center.

When I pulled up, I was immediately approached by two dope boys that started arguing over which one of them was gonna serve me. I quickly let them both know that I didn't need any of whatever it was that they were selling. Then the ugliest, dirtiest looking one proceeded to try and get his holla on. His breath smelled like straight, weed and hot ass. I politely declined his attempt to holla.

About a minute or so later, Pleasure came out of what appeared to be a crack-house. She was all hoochied out, like she was on her way to the club or something. She had on some leggings and a jersey dress with a pair of hi-heels. And she had a Miami-Maxx fleece hoodie wrapped around her shoulders. For some reason, this whole thing had Boom-Boom written all over it.

"What's up, girl?" I asked as Pleasure jumped into the car and shut the door without responding.

"Can I ask what you are doing in Overtown?" I asked as we drove through the hood as fast as possible, to try and avoid being jacked.

"Can you just take me home?" Pleasure mumbled.

"Okay. But, are you gonna tell me what you doing in a Overtown at this time of the night?" I asked in a more expectant tone of voice.

"Okay. I was chillin' wit Boom at the dog fight in the old warehouse. After the fight, everybody was hangin out, parking lot pimpin', just kickin' it. Then Mikey Tidwell came up to say hi and give me a hug. The next thing I knew Boom-Boom had dude on the ground pistol whippin' him for nothing, after that he took the back of his hand and slapped the taste outta my mouth. When I fell down he started kickin' me, and yellin' something about reckless eye-ballin' and dispectin' a pimp. I can't believe he would do me like that in front of all those people." (Pleasure paused) "I'm hurt bad, Angell! How am I gonna go to the funeral lookin' like this?" She said as she started to cry. And then she pulled her hood off and turned toward me. I almost wrecked Chance's car!

Her face was all bruised and bloody. Her top lip was busted and her eye swollen shut. Pleasure looked like Frankenstein's monster. I pulled over at a liquor store.

"Oh my God! Oh my God! Girl, what did that nigga do to you? We gotta get you to a hospital!" I screamed in horror at her almost disfigured face.

"Please! No, just take me home! If I show up at a hospital like this, word will be all over Miami by in the morning. Please just take me home!" Pleasure sobbed over and over again.

"Okay! But as soon as we get there, we are calling the police! That nigga is going to jail tonite!" I shouted as I recklessly sped down Biscayne, my eyes filled with tears.

"The police? Are you crazy? Do you know who you are talkin' about? Do you think that I'm actually about to press charges against Big-Mann's bother? And just which one of the one hundred and some odd people that were there tonight is gonna testify against him, and admit to being at an illegal dogfight? That nigga is crazy! He beat me to a pulp in front of everybody.

His cousin Tasheen picked me up, put me in her car and took me back to her mama's house in Overtown. That's where I called you from. I just wanna go home," Pleasure pleaded again.

So, I took her home. When we got to the house, it was completely silent. My father was asleep. I opened the door and cut off the alarm. We walked inside and headed straight to the kitchen, so I could try to clean her up and put some ice on her face. But before we could make it, Pleasure started throwin' up all over the floor.

I got her into the kitchen and sat her down. Then, I paused and sniffed her clothes.

"Girl, you smell like weed! What have you been doing? And that vomit on the floor smells like liquor! What were you doing tonite?" I demanded.

"I just had one or two drinks, maybe three at the most. And I only hit the blunt once or twice, that was it! I swear! It ain't no big deal!" Pleasure mumbled through her busted upper lip.

"I should finish kickin' yo' butt myself! Pleasure you are a gospel music singer! That technically means that you are a minister of the gospel and people look up to you. Why would you be drinkin' and gettin' high?" I was out done! I tried to stop myself before I even got started.

Pleasure ran and threw up again in the kitchen sink. I just shook my head. Then I walked her to her room, helped her get undressed and into bed. I stayed with her to make sure that she was okay Because of the beatin' she took, I wanted to keep an eye on her. So I called Chance and let him know what happened and that I would be spending the night at home.

The next morning I got up and went into the kitchen to put on a pot of coffee, I knew lil' Ms. Hot Pants would need it once she came to. As I commenced to cleaning up her mess, my father walked in. He gasped in surprise and put his arms around me. "Beanpole!" he shouted as he hugged me. I slowly and hesitantly returned his embrace.

"I'm sorry, Beanpole, I didn't mean to hurt you! I'm really sorry! And I don't blame you for being mad, but please don't hate me! I love you, Beanpole!" My father said as he held me in his arms tighter and more sincerely then he ever had before. My heart began to melt.

"I Love you, too Daddy! I might not like you very much right now, but I still love you." I said as we hugged. I knew that if I was gonna get through this day at all. I had to first make peace with my father. I breathed a strange sign of relief.

"I'm sorry about Vartan. I don't know what to say" my father struggled for words as he sat down at the kitchen table and rubbed his face, "It's for the best though, I knew he wasn't right for you, but I would have never figured him for a murderer", my father commented.

"Yeah, me either. Well, I'm gonna get ready, so we can get to the funeral. We don't wanna be Late." I said, as Pleasure came in to the kitchen holding her bruised face. My father turned around to look at Pleasure.

"What in the devil happened to you? My father shouted as he stared at Pleasure's busted face in horror. But I don't know what he was all excited about. She didn't look half as bad as she did the night before. Pleasure tried to explain to my father what had happened. But the more she explained, the madder and more disgusted he got.

"I tried to tell you about that little thug a long time ago. But you wouldn't listen; you just couldn't seem to stay away from him. Now he's beatin' on you! Look at yourself! Do you see what sneaking around and being hard headed has gotten you? I gotta get ready. The limousine from the funeral home will be here in about an hour. Let's not keep him waiting" my father said as he got up and walked away to go get dressed. Pleasure and I did the same.

CHAPTER 17

When the limo got there, we all got in and headed to the funeral. The ride there was completely silent. Nobody said a word or made any eye contact. My father was all decked out in his black custom fitted Armani suit (still looking like an old ass Denzel Washington), Pleasure wore a stunning two piece suit by Dior that was the cut to the thigh, with a black Panama Fedora hat that had a sheer black vale to hide her tears and her bruises.

When we got there the church was packed, every deacon, preacher and prophet in Florida had come to say goodbye to my mother. She did a lot for a lot of people, and the air was filled with love.

As we made our way up to the front of the church to be seated, I saw Chance. He sat toward the middle right by the isle. We made eye contact and smiled at each other. Pleasure stared at Chance through her black veil. Chance couldn't help but notice Pleasure because of the way that Black Dior suit hugged every curve in her shape. She caused every man in the church to take notice.

Sister Walls gave the eulogy. Then my father got up and said a few words. Pleasure was suppose to sing, but that wasn't gonna happen, for obvious reasons.

I thought I wouldn't make it through that day. But surprisingly having, Chance, my father and Pleasure by my side made every difference in the world. And having Chance's support really helped to lift my spirits. But my faith in God is really what carried me. There was no way that I could have made it with out him.

After the funeral, everybody came back to our house to show their condolences. Chance got there right after we did. I introduced him to my father. Pleasure had already seen Chance but she had never actually met him, so I introduced her as well. I could see her meat hooks come out. Her mouth started to water at the sight of Chance. But I wasn't worried because although Pleasure was a man-eater I knew that she would never do anything to hurt me. And she knew that I was really feeling Chance.

Beside that, Pleasure had her hands full. About an hour after we got there, Big-Mann showed up to pay his respects, and right behind him was Boom-Boom and his new bodyguard, J-Fire.

Pleasure caught sight of Boom-Boom and froze instantly, as if she had seen a vicious pit-bull without a leash and there was nothing between them but space and opportunity.

Boom Boom looked over at Pleasure. Pleasure look at my father. My father looked over at Big Mann. Big-Mann smirked and tapped Boom on the shoulder, then whispered something into his ear. Boom-Boom blew Pleasure a kiss and walked back out of the door.

My father motioned to Big Mann, who followed him down the hall in to the study. Pleasure hurried away into her room and closed the door; curiosity had gotten the best of me.

I excused myself from Chance and told him that I had to use the restroom. Then, I casually walked down the hall and into my parent's room, so that I could eaves drop. I closed the door and pressed my ear to the wall to listen.

"I'm gonna get right to the point. We've made a lot money together over the last few years. I've scratched yo' back, and you've scratched mine. But now I need something extra from you, a really huge favor. I need for you to find away to get me on the church board and make me treasurer, so that I can start laundering some of this dope money through the churches accounts. I know that the treasurer's seat is open. And I want it! I need you to make it happen, like yesterday" Big Mann demanded.

"What? Are you crazy? I can't do that! I won't! What will people say?" My father shouted. I struggled to hear with my ear still pressed against the bedroom wall.

"Don't get cute! Did I ask questions when you needed dear old Mrs. Trenton outta the way so you could gain control over her property, and make yo' little deal with the city? That made you a rich man. Did I say no to you then? You know it would be damn ashamed if anybody ever found out what really happened to Pleasure's granny! Now, you had me kill that old woman and then you practically sold her granddaughter to me. Now that's some real life pimpin right there!" Big-Mann paused.

"Oh, Pleasure. Dear, sweet, juicy little Pleasure, me and that little ho' done made some beautiful music together, in more ways than one. HA! HA! That pussy sho' is good! (Big-Mann laughed) "I'm just kiddin" Big-Mann pulled a napkin from his pocket and wiped the sweat from his shiny baldhead.

"That girl really is a pleasure though. And you've made quite a bit of money off her too, haven't you, Pastor? I'd hate for anybody to find out what really happened to her granny! Wouldn't you?" Big-Mann said as he continued to chuckle cold-heartedly.

"Don't chu' threaten me! I didn't have anything to do with that old lady's death! Your bother and his thugs killed her! And you paid the fire marshal to say that was accident", my father whispered. I gasped in disbelief.

"Yeah but you ordered the hit. You wanted that land, and the old lady was holding up progress for you and yo' so called church, which is really nothing more than a cash cow. And now, I want in on it. I want some of that cow!" Big-Mann said as he lit a cigar.

"You have some nerve coming here on the day of my wife's funeral!", my father said.

"Oh, cut the act! You didn't give a damn about yo' wife! You been bonin' Sister Brant, Sister East and Reverend Serls wife for years now. But what else could you do after finding out that yo' wife was a lesbian?" I slid to the floor in shock as Big-Mann continued his verbal assault on my father. "Oh, you didn't think that her and Sister Walls were just prayer partners, did you? (Big-Mann laughed out loud) It burned you up didn't it? To know that yo' wife was getting mo' pussy than you were, but at least she had the sense to be discreet with it! Unlike you!" Big-Mann said, as he turned his back.

"You fat mutha...." My father growled, as Big-Mann cut him off.

"Ya' know, me and you are really two of a kind. Yeah, we both some pimps. The only difference between us is, I trick my ho's out using dope and money. But you trick yo' ho's out using the bible. Now that takes some serious, serious game" (Big-Mann took another puff from his cigar) "I'll give you two weeks to take care of the details with the church board. Please make sure that I get a nice big office too, I'm big man." Big-Mann said as he laughed again and walked out of my father's study and pimped back through the house past all the church folks. Then he stopped, and turned to look at Pleasure.

"Make sure you're on time for the studio tomorrow. Boom will be here to get you at twelve o'clock, be ready! You know how short his patience can be." Big-Mann said as he provokingly looked around at all the church folks before he walked out of the door.

I couldn't believe what I had just heard. It had to be a lie. It must have been. But there was nobody in that room but them two. So Big-mann didn't have any reason to lie. And my father never denied a word of what Big-Mann was saying.

But I still didn't believe it. I know my father could not have had anything to do with Mrs. Trenton's death. And I was never going to believe that my mother had been having a lesbian affair with Sister Walls! I was never gonna accept that!

I was shocked beyond belief. I was so confused. I didn't know what to do. I didn't know whether to go in and comfort father or confront my father. I was already mad as hell at him for cheatin' on my mother, but now to find out that he also might be involved in the murder of

Pleasure's grandma. I could hardly hold myself together.

Pleasure was still a mess from the night before, so she went back and hid herself in her room. We had decided to tell everybody that she fell off her bike, even though her face looked more like she had fallen out of an airplane. She was a nervous wreck and having Boom-Boom show up at our house with Big Mann didn't make things any better.

After Big-Mann left, my father walked over to two of the other associates minister that sat on the board of trustees. He whispered something in both their ears, and they looked each at other anxiously. The two of them stood nervously off to the side while my father showed all the rest of the people out.

Once everybody was gone, my father and the two other ministers excused themselves and headed down the hall to my father's study. My father stopped and kissed me on my forehead as he left the room. I could barely stand to look at him. I was sick to my stomach thinking about everything I'd just heard.

Chance sat quietly on the sofa, and waited patiently for me. I sat down on the arm of the couch next to him. He reached over and touched my hand, I couldn't stop shaking. He stood up and put his arms around me. Right there I almost went to pieces.

I knew that I had to get out of that house immediately or I was going to lose my mind. I told Chance to get ready so that we could leave. I raced around the house trying to grab everything that I thought I would need. I had the feeling that I was gonna be gone for awhile.

I packed all of my bags, went in and told Pleasure that I was leaving. She hugged me and said that she understood, but made me promise to say in touch with her.

I grabbed Chance by the hand and walked over to the door, stopping for just a moment to look down the hallway toward my father's office. Apart of me wanted to go run and put my arms around him. Another part of me wanted to walk away from him and never look back.

I had decided to go back home with Chance until I got my mind together. I wasn't in any shape to make any real decisions other than that.

So, I put my bags in the back of Chance's Range Rover, kissed him on his check and told him that I would be right behind him. I still had his BMW and had to drive it back to his house. I was going to come back later in the week to get my car and some more of my stuff.

Pleasure came outside and stood in front of the house as I prepared to go. She asked me if there was anything that I wanted her to tell my father. I just told her to tell him that I would call him in a few days and that I loved him. Then I got into the car and followed Chance up the road.

CHAPTER 18

It was raining cats and dogs, as it had been doing all week. The roads were terrible. I could hardly see 20 yards in front of me. I hated driving in the rain, but we didn't have far to go.

I had packed my glasses away inside one of my bags, and I wasn't wearing my contacts. I didn't normally need them, except for reading and driving night driving and it was only dusk, so I figured I was okay to make to the beach house.

The silence of the drive was making me a little edgy, so I reached down to turn on the stereo. I thought maybe some music might help to get my mind off things. I flipped through a few stations until I found something that I could listen to. Ironically they were playing Keyshia Cole's song "Sent From Heaven". I was really feeling that! I looked ahead at Chance who was driving in front of me and I smiled. The words to her song connected with me instantly.

For a second, I actually even I thought of his kisses and his touch. I had never felt that way before and I knew that whether I liked it or not, I was falling in love. Which was crazy, because the whole world had started to crumble around me, but Chance was right there to pick up my broken pieces.

After Keyshia Cole finished wailing, the radio started playing something by some rock group, with guitars blaring, and voices screeching. I quickly reached down to change the tuner but I couldn't find anything that I wanted to hear. So I looked up into the visor to see what C'Ds Chance had, then all the disks came falling out into my lap. I looked down at the CD's really quickly, only taking my eyes off the road for a second.

When I looked back up something had darted out into the middle of the road. It looked like a dog or something. I blew the horn to try and scare it out of my way, but it wouldn't move. So, I quickly swerved to avoid it and lost control of the car. I went into a 180-degree spin. When I came to a stop the car was facing the wrong way on the road.

Chance saw what happened and stopped immediately, putting his car into reverse. He backed up toward me and got out. I was in shock, but grateful to be alive.

I press down on the clutch, and turned the key, but the ignition had stalled. I turned the key again but there was no use, I guess I had flooded the engine. And to make matter worse, just over the hill ahead of me, the reflection of two blinding headlights sparkled against the pouring rain.

There was a car coming straight toward me just beyond the hill. And once they got over that ridge there was no way that they were gonna be able to stop. They were going to plow right into me.

I could see the lights getting brighter as they got closer. The vehicle was now in full sight as it reached the top of the ridge. It was a huge SUV and they were only about 50 yards away and moving at least forty-five to fifty miles per hour. They would have needed to hit the brakes right then in order to avoid smashing into me, but they didn't even see me.

Their headlights grew more and more intense until I was almost blinded. The driver of the large white SUV must have finally caught sight of me, because they quickly slammed on their brakes. They swerved and hit a huge slick in the road as they began to hydroplane, spinning out of control and slamming sideways into a tree. The front of the vehicle was completely detached from the rest of body. The horn was stuck and blaring loudly into the night.

I instantly started to pray for all the people in the wreaked truck as I frantically dialed 911.

The cabin of the truck was on it's top by the side of the road, smashed up against the tree. Who ever was inside started to scream as the truck burst in flames. There was smoke everywhere.

Chance ran over to the accident. The heat grew more and more intense as he got closer. He tried to shield his face with his forearm as he kicked in the window on the driver side. Chance struggled to get the driver out. The man was bleeding from a huge gash in his head caused by a tree branch that come through the window during the crash.

Chance rushed around to the other side of the truck to free the passengers. He forced the door open and pulled each of them out by the road. He checked both the other men's pulse but they were already dead.

Chance ran back over to the driver to try and stop the bleeding from his head. He recognized the man from earlier that day at my mother's funeral, it was Big Mann's bodyguard J-Fire. He was unconscious but he was alive.

Chance walked back over to me and fell against the car, exhausted from the heat and fumes. I put my arms around him and grabbed my cell phone to call the police again, but I hung up as I heard them already coming over the ridge.

When the paramedics and police got there they lit the whole place up with flashing lights. It was actually the first opportunity I had to see the scene clearly. And it was horrible.

There were parts of their truck everywhere. I glanced at the license plate that hung by one screw from the twisted metal bumper. It said "BIG MAN8". The truck belonged to Big-Mann. He was the person that Chance removed from the passenger's seat. And the other man in the back of the SUV was his brother Boom-Boom. They were both pronounced dead at the scene. Jay-Fire, the bodyguard was rushed to the hospital.

I couldn't believe it. I was in total shock. I immediately called Pleasure to tell her what had happened but she never answered. So I said that I would just call and talk to her when I got back to Chance's.

Despite what had happened between her & Boom the day before, I knew that she was going to take the news of his death pretty hard. So I wanted to be there for her.

The wreckage was removed from the road and the debris was cleared. The police interviewed us about the accident and we told them all that we could, which wasn't much. Then we both got back in ours cars and continued on to Chance's house.

CHAPTER 19

When we got home we made our way inside and into the sitting room where we had last been together. Chance sat down on the sofa. I sat beside him and laid my head against his chest. He put his arms around me. I shook my head in total disbelief about everything that had happened. I was about ready to come apart at the seams but Chance gave me the comfort I needed to at least get through that moment. And that was really all that I could do, is take it moment by moment.

Both Chance and I were completely exhausted. So we decided to get ready for bed and call it a night.

I got up and headed upstairs to change my clothes and take a shower. Once I finshed, I went back into my room to lay down across the bed. I was wiped out. The events of the day had taken everything from me. I was so tried but I dared not close my eyes to sleep in fear of what dreams might come.

Chance came upstairs and went into the bathroom. I heard him turn the shower on. So I got up, walked into the hallway, and stood outside by the bathroom. The door was slightly open.

The steam from the shower seeped out as Chance's fragrant body wash summoned me in. My fingers trembled as I raised my hand to push the open wider.

The lights were dimmed but I could see the silhouette of Chance's body through the mist on the glass. I slowly stepped inside and stood silently at the doorway. I felt the hot vapors against my skin as I was still only wearing a towel.

I moved closer inside. Chance paused. He didn't say anything but I could tell that he knew I was there.

A nervous rush ran through me as I dropped my towel on the floor and walked over toward the shower. The steam over whelmed me or maybe it was my nerves.

Step, by step I moved closer. Chance turned toward me. I could sense him looking at me through the defused glass. I wanted to say his name, call him out loud, but I couldn't speak.

Chance also wanted to call out to me but not to ask why I was there, because he knew why I was there and he knew what I wanted. I was there for him. I wanted him. I needed him to touch me. My heart was broken in seventeen different places and I needed him to take his hands and put me back together again.

I took another step, trying to cover my breast but I wanted Chance to see me. I wanted to be naked before him. I wanted him to see all that I was.

I rose my other arm toward the handle on the shower door, but before I could reach it, Chance slid the glass door open wide. The steam from the hot water almost hid him from my sight. But then I saw him fully.

He was gorgeous! His body beautiful and strong. I had never been this close to a man's unclothed body before. I had never even allowed myself to imagine it.

The sight of his masculine figure almost caused my heart to stop, my knees went weak and I fell backward. But Chance stepped forward and grabbed me. He picked me up into his arms. We stood silently for a few short moments. He looked at me, studying my nakedness from head to toe.

I reached my hand toward his face. I ached to touch him but I didn't dare, because I knew that once I held him in my grasp, letting go would no longer be an option.

My hand shook as I inched closer with my fingertips. His lip, his eyes, and his smooth baldhead all made me his prisoner.

He was still wet with steamy water droplets all over his body. I couldn't believe where I was or what I was doing. Nobody would have believed it. But there I was, naked inside the arms of this black Adonis.

Finally, I couldn't resist anymore. I touched his face and kissed his beautiful full lips. I breathed him in.

Chance carried me from the bathroom into his bedroom, laying me down. There was a small awkward moment of silence, and then Chance laid beside me. He kissed my lips again, deeply and passionately I touched his chest and his broad shoulders as his hands glided over every inch of my body.

Chance got on top of me. I grabbed his baldhead as he kissed my neck and chest. The tension mounted between us as he moved his kisses farther down, gently licking and pulling at my nipples, again and again and again until goose bumps cover my entire body. My head began to spin like I was on the tea-cup ride at Disney world.

Chance was driving me crazy teasing my titties. I finally couldn't take it anymore and I had to push him off. Then he started to move down. My stomach muscles flexed and tightened as he kissed me. My pussy was gushing wet, like it had been since I saw him standing there in the shower.

I had never done anything like this before. I had never been touched like this or kissed the way that Chance kissed me. And I had never ever allowed myself to become aroused this way. I was throbbing! Chance had me simmering in my own juices.

My legs shook as he softly kissed just below my waist and around my hips. His touch was tender and sweet. I felt a slight chill from the cool evening air as Chance continued downward with his kisses and slowly began to part my thighs.

He gently pressed his soft lips against the top of my pussy. My clit was pulsating! My heart raced out of control but in prefect time with his every touch. I shuttered as he breathed on my skin. And then my entire body seized and quaked as he place his mouth over my lips and began to lick and suck me ever so softly, taking his time to taste me completely.

Over and over again Chance teased me. One time after another he would bring me to edge of climax but then pull me away from the edge. Time after time he brought me to brink of ecstasy, until I finally exploded.

I laid there speechless as Chance stood over me, fully erect. A cold sweat dampened me all over as I trembled. I was out of control.

I couldn't stop my legs from shaking. Chance had taken me to a place that I never even knew existed. I had never ever felt such a sweet sensation. And I had never been so confused.

I was in heaven, but I knew I was going to hell. I always promised my mother that I would save my body for the man I married. And that I would wait to have sex until God said that it was right.

But I had fallen into temptation and broken my solemn vow to my mother, to myself and above all, to God.

I immediately turned over and hurried to cover my body with a sheet. Chance reached out to touch me, but I pulled away. I couldn't even look at him. I quickly got up and ran back into the guest room and shut the door.

I was so ashamed. I fell down on my knees to pray and beg God for his forgiveness. But I couldn't find the words.

I knew that I loved Chance but I loved God more. I rolled over and closed my eyes and tried sleep but my conscience would not have it.

About an hour or so went by and I kept thinking about my mother, and my father, and Pleasure and Chance. Everything seemed to flood my emotions all at once. I was overwhelmed by all that had happened over the last couple of weeks, and I still wasn't sure if Pleasure had heard about Big-Mann & Boom, so I called her.

When she picked up the phone, I could tell that she was still awake and that she had been crying, she had already found out the news.

She wondered what I was still doing up at 2:30 in the morning. I told her that I couldn't sleep. And apparently she couldn't sleep either.

I asked her how she was doing after hearing about Big-Mann and Boom Boom. She was really sort of quiet on the subject and didn't seem to want to talk, which was a bit odd, but I tried to understand.

Pleasure had been secretly seeing Boom-Boom for years. Their relationship was more of an on again off kind of thing, but as far as boyfriends went, Boom-Boom was probably the closest thing she had. And what was crazy is, nobody really knew about it but me.

I was the one who would cover for her when would sneak out to be with him. I knew that he was no good, but she would always tell me to mind my own business whenever I tried to warn her.

She was crazy over him from the start. I always believed that it was her fooling around with him that got her grandma killed. That is, until I heard the conversation between my father and Big-Mann. Then I didn't know what to believe.

I was so torn up and confused. I couldn't even tell Pleasure about what I had over heard, not until I knew for sure. Because not only did Big-Mann implicate Boom-Boom in her grandma's murder but he also implicated my father. So I had to be certain of what I was saying before I told anybody, even Chance.

Pleasure asked if I was okay, I wanted to tell her yes but I couldn't force the lie from my lips. And anyway, she knew that I was far from being okay. I just couldn't tell her everything yet.

I asked her how my father was and if he had already gone to bed. She told me that he had gone to the hospital to be with Big-Mann's mother, she was another longtime member of our church. She was actually the one who help groom Pleasure and helped Big-Mann to get his gospel music label off the ground.

Her and Pleasure never really got along. She always thought that Pleasure was too fast, and that she was always trying to flaunt her body in front of men. But she had her nerve talking about anybody, because this lady was know as the oldest freak in the church. I personally always thought that she just jealous of Pleasure.

Before we hung up, I apologized to Pleasure again for the mean things I had said. I also let her know that I really was sorry about Boom-Boom's death, but gladly she was taking it a lot better that n it thought she would. Pleasure was about the closest thing I had ever had to a sister, and even with all her faults she was still family.

CHAPTER 20

The following day I had gotten up early to talk to Chance. But when I went to check his room he had already gone. I tried his cell phone but there was no answer. So I decide to take a walk on the beach until he got back.

But before I could get out of the door my cell phone rang. It was Selvan Scaggs, a friend of mine from high school. He worked for the Miami-Dade Police. His mother was also a member of the church.

He was calling about the accident last night. Selvan said that he had something really important to tell me, and he asked if we could meet somewhere later that morning.

I was a little hesitant but even more curious. So, I agreed to meet him at The China Grill down on Washington Avenue. I had some business to take care near there anyway, so I figured that I could see Selvan, get some lunch and then go run my errands.

When I arrived at the restaurant Selvan was already there, he was seated in the back. I walked over to the table. I could tell by the expression on his face that what ever he had to tell me must have been really heavy. He stood up and greeted me with a hug and a kiss on the cheek.

"I'm sorry about your mom. I wanted to be there for the funeral but I got stuck workin' a detail. I couldn't get out of it!" Selvan said as he touched my hand.

"It's fine. I know, I talked to your mom" I responded as I took my purse off my shoulder and sat down at the table.

"I want to talk to you about the incident you saw last night with Tony Biggs and his brother. I'm actually assisting in the murder investigate," He said staring straight at me as I was taken completely off gurard.

"Murder! What Murder?" I asked.

"Angell, the accident you saw last night wasn't what actually killed Big-Mann and Boom." He said with his eyes still trained on mine, as I sipped my lemon water.

"What are you saying, Selvan?" I asked.

"They were both murdered", Selvan responded.

"What do you mean Murdered? Chance pulled them all out of the truck. It was an accident! I saw the crash!" I said in shock.

"They both died from gunshot wounds. They were shot in the back, at point back range before that accident. They were executed." Selvan said as he shifted in his seat never loosing eye contact for a second.

"But how? Chance would have noticed the blood! Especially from a gun shot wound!" I comment. "And what about the driver? Was he shot too?" I inquired, replaying the scene in my head as he spoke.

"That's the interesting thing" He said reaching into his stylish brown leather Gucci brief case. Selvan was a very handsome and well put together light skinned brotha', too bad he was gay.

"Angel, do you remember about ten years ago, when that girl and her four kids got killed in Overtown? It was the summer before we started junior high school. Her name was

Javette Reynolds.", he asked, pulling out an old newspaper clipping'

"Yeah, I remember. I remember quite well!" I responded solemnly, recounting the day my mother and I visited her and her kids.
"The driver of the truck that night was Javette's younger brother. He was Big Mann's driver and bodyguard his name was Jayvin Reynolds. He's the one who pulled the trigger on Big-Mann and Boom." He said as he continued to look through his bag.

"Okay, so what's this have to do with me?" I asked, as I started to get somewhat uneasy.

"He's said that your father paid him $50,000 to do it. He says your dad set the whole thing up" Selvan said as he began to almost cut through me with his stare. I almost fell out of my seat.

"That's ridiculous! Why would my father want either one of them dead?" I ask. But I had a real good idea about why he would want them both dead or at least I thought I did.

"Angel, I don't know if you realize this but, your father has been involved in some pretty questionable activities over the past few years.

The Miami Dade Police has had him under investigation for some time now, because of his connection with Big-Mann and some other major crime figures. The record company that he helped start was just a money laundering front. And according to Jayvin, who's been working inside Big-Mann's organization for over a year now, Big Mann's been black mailing your father. Apparently his demand's started to become too much, your father came to Jayvin (who goes by the street name J-Fire) and made him an offer to take care of Big Mann. Which wasn't a hard sell, considering the fact that the only reason that Jayvin was even working for Big-Mann anyway was to get close enough to him to get revenge for the death of his sister and her children. Big-Mann never even realized who Jayvin (or J-Fire as they called him) was." He said as I sat totally stunned by what I had just been told, but I had not heard anything yet!

"But why did he kill Boom-Boom?", I asked as if it really made any differences.

"Well, that's simple. Boom and his crew, The Knock Off Boyz, were actually the assassins that killed J-Fire's sister and her kids, so, killing Boom was just an extra treat." Selvan said as I sat stone faced and stunned. I wanted to cry but after all I had been through, there weren't any tears left.

"The crime scene investigators found this inside the truck. It was turned in to me. It doesn't have any real bearing on the case, but the department is releasing it to the press tomorrow. I tried to get them not to but, there was nothing I could do." He said as he reached inside the bag and handed me a DVD disk.

"What is this?" I asked, with most incredible sense of dread I had ever felt before.

"It's a..." Sylvan struggled as he started to weep. "It's something that I wish I could have made go away, but I can't. But it's something that you outta see before the rest of Miami gets their hands on it." He said as he grabbed his briefcase, quickly stood to his feet, wiped his eyes and walked away.

I picked up the disk, put it away inside my purse and made my way out of restaurant.

A few moments later I got in the car and started to make my way back to Hibiscus Island. But something made me go the other way. So I jumped on I95 and before I knew it, I was on NW 67th ST. headed toward 14th AVE. I was back in Overtown, by our old house. I pulled up and sat outside, and watched people come and go. They were just ordinary people, without fancy cars or big houses.

But they seemed happy, even without all the material trappings that many of them probably wished for, the things that some of them even plotted, schemed and hustle for.

I thought back on the days when we reached out to the hungry and ministered to the hurting from the small church house across the street.

Before we got all high sidity and moved out of the hood, before the business of tithes and offering turned into just a business, when we sometimes fed our neighbors right out of our own cabinets and refrigerator.

When all we had was fifteen or twenty faithful members, before we had a building that seated ten thousand. When our small, humble church was still a church. When the smell of the ghetto was still fresh on our clothes.

But those days were gone, and what use to be was now dead, the true sprit of God had left us because of all our phony pretenses, and from this, there seemed to be no turning back.

CHAPTER 21

As the day began to turn into dusk, I arrived back at Chance's beach house. He was out on the deck grilling baby-back ribs and chicken.

I walked out and gave him a hug, falling into his arms as I had grown so accustomed to doing over the last few weeks. I wanted to tell him some many things but my mouth wouldn't form the words. So, I went back into the house and walked into living room where I saw the disk sticking out that Selvan had given me at the restaurant.

I knew that I had to watch that disk, but I had the worst feeling about it. Like, when you were a kid, and you were up late getting ready to watch a blood horror film that you knew was going to give you nightmares for weeks and months afterward. This was the same terrible feeling I had about what I was getting ready to see.

I held the DVD in my hand, I put it in the player, but I was afraid to let it go. But I knew that I had to. So I pushed in, turned the TV on. I was not prepared for what I was about to see.

When the video came on, it was kind of dark and fuzzy, real amateur quality. But as it came into focus it showed Vartan sitting on a couch with a drink in hand. He was laughing and talking loud and there was loud rap music playing in the background. Then who ever was holding the camera started saying something like," There It is"

And then, the camera went slightly out of focus again. But it came back.

Then it panned over to what I guess was the bedroom, and coming out of the door, dancing and stripping to the music, was Dilonda Lovetts, the girl that Vartan murdered. She was wearing nothing but a g-string, she walked over and started bumpin' and grindin' all on Vartan.

And then the camera went out of focus again and panned back around to the bedroom door, where another girl came out dancing. When the camera came back into focus, there was Pleasure.

She was wearing a black two piece lingerie set with the matching garter. She also walked over to Vartan and started lap dancing for him as he smacked her on her ass.

Then the person that was holding the camera sat it down and walked passed the lens. I could feel myself begin to gag.

There was my father standing there with his shirt opened, dancing and clownin' with a drink and a blunt in his hand. He went over to the love seat and sat down, while Vartan's nasty baby mama took off her g-string and gave him a buttnekket lap dance.

Vartan had Pleasure bent over on the couch with her top off, as she did that nasty stripper booty clap dance. I almost threw up!

Then she walked over to my father, got on her knees in front of him and started to unzip his pants. I quickly shut the TV off before I could see anymore. I was numb all over.

I turned around to see Chance standing behind me in the doorway. He had seen everything. I was broken. I felt that everything had now taken from me.

I walked over to Chance and just stood. And then the room went dark. I fainted in his arms. When I woke up I was upstairs. He was right next to me when I opened my eyes.

I sat up all night just staring out of the window. Chance sat up with me. We didn't say a word. There wasn't anything to say.

My mother was gone, and my man had betrayed me, my so called sister and best friend had been fucking my father and my man for who knows how long. And in about twelve hours, what was left of my life was getting ready to be torn down in front of the whole city of Miami. I had lost everything. The vulchers were circling overhead and I wasn't even dead yet.

Chance and I watched the sun come up. It was beautiful. It was the first sunny day I had seen in a while. It seemed like it had been raining forever. Or maybe I was just stuck underneath a dark cloud.

When Chance's alarm clock rang he got up, kissed my forehead went into his room to turn it off.

I went downstairs to make Chance some breakfast. I cut the television on in the kitchen; I set it to channel 3 because I wanted to check the weather.

But instead of the day's forecast, here's what I got.

"Good morning, this is Wu-Ty-Ching, reporting live from Coral Gables. I'm outside the First New Worship Center to bring you a story that you'll only see here on News Center 3.

On Monday of this week we reported to you on a bizarre traffic accident that resulted in two fatalities and one person left in serious but stable condition.

Apparently the two people that were thought to have died as a result of that crash had actually been murder. According the coroner's report they both died from gunshot wounds that they sustained earlier. The driver of the vehicle was apparently on his way to dump the bodies in the Everglade Reserve National Park.

This is where the story takes a really strange twist. The driver reportedly gave a sworn taped statement to police that he was paid by the Pastor of this local church to murder Anthony Biggs, known as Big-Mann, who has as extensive criminal history and was also under federal investigation for aggravated drug trafficking and money laundering.

Now if you think that's bizarre, wait until you hear this. Early this morning a video was anonymously delivered to our studios, this video allegedly shows the pastor of this church, Winfred Epps, participating in some sort of sex orgy with two women. Pastor Epps, along with Vartan Daniels, quarterback for the Miami Maxx are both allegedly in this video drinking alcohol and smoking marijuana.

Vartan Daniel is currently being held in Cincinnati, Ohio for the murder of one of the women on the video, also reported to be the mother of his child.

The other woman in the video is reported to be gospel singer, Pleasure Trenton.

This is certainly one strange and incredibly complicated story but we'll bring you more information as it becomes available.

This is Wu-Ty-Ching reporting for News-Center-3. Now, back to you Stacey", the beautiful Asian news reporter said as I leaned against the counter in the center of the kitchen. I felt like I had just been sucker punched by a super-heavy weight champion in the 10th round.

I was beyond tired, I was worn out, finished. This was the last straw. There was no more that I could stand. I felt like walking out into the ocean. I was too exhausted to go on and too tired to even quit, but the prospect of death seemed more appealing with each moment that passed.

Then just like clock work the clouds came back. The sky returned itself to dark and the wind began to blow from the ocean. I shook my head in disbelief at my outrageous misfortune. The sun fought to shine but the overcast took over.

I turned off the fire on the stove and walked over to the sliding glass door. I turned the lock and pulled the door open. A crisp sea breeze met me instantly as I stepped out on to the deck. I took a deep breath, walked over to the heavy wooden railing and stood still.

I remember a gospel song that my mother always sang when she was sad, it said
Sometimes he calms the storm with a whisper, peace be still. He can settle any sea, but it doesn't mean he will. Sometime he holds us close and let's the wind and waves go wild. Sometimes he calms the storm and other times

he calms his child." So, even though the storms of life were raging all around me I decided to stand still and hold close to GOD. What else could I do?

I mean, I was so hurt, on so many levels. The man that I planned to marry had been playing me for a fool, I could have been with so many different guys that were so much better than him. I guess he thought that just because he had money he could do whatever the hell he wanted to do to people, but now look where he is.

And Pleasure, I mean, this tramp, this lil' orphan Annie ass bitch, with nothing, came to live with me and my parents. I shared everything with her, even my mother's love! Now to find out that she has probably been fucking my father and my fiancé for years. I wanted to go over to that house and bust her damn head to the white meat! But in stead, I STOOD STILL and put it into GOD's hands.

CHAPTER 22

The early autumn rains continued to fall as I stood outside on the wood deck staring at the ocean with tears in my eyes. I watched the waves crash against the sandy shoreline of the beach as the wind began to pick up. It was hurricane season in Miami, in more ways than one.

From behind me, I heard the sound of the glass patio door slide open. It was Chance. I heard his footsteps move toward me, but I never turned around. I didn't want him to see that I had been crying again, but he didn't need to see my face, because he knew when I was hurting. It seemed like he could just feel it!

Chance walked up and stood right behind me. With my back still turned he put his arms around my waist and held me close. As he softly kissed the back of my neck and shoulders a heavenly chill went down my spine. He had never touched me this way before! His hands were warm and strong. His kisses were tender and sweet. I was comforted instantly. His touch sent a rush all the way through me that made my whole body hot! I had been waiting for this for so long!

I turned around to face him. Then, with out even so much as a single word, he slowly pressed his soft, full lips against mine. I reached up and slid the tips of my fingers against his smooth baldhead while the rain washed over us both. His powerful arms tightened down around me like two steel bands that I could not have escaped even if I had wanted to, which I didn't, not even in the least!

Slowly I ran my hands underneath his soaking wet tank top as the rain started to pour and he squeezed me even tighter. Our eyes locked as the wind blew and the storm brewed around us! I touched his chest and proceeded to slide my hands all over his hard, muscular frame. His pecks rippled and flexed as he lifted me up on to the wooden guard railing, kissing and biting me on the neck, while I grew hotter and hotter!

Then he wrapped his fist around the collar of my t-shirt and ripped it straight down the middle, exposing both of my breasts. He held them in his hands and licked the droplets of rain from my nipples. I was under his complete control! I put my arms around his neck as he tore my panties apart at the seams and snatched them off of me. He put his arms back around me and kissed me deeply as I reached down into his shorts. I gasped as I touched his manhood. It was so long and so hard! "Hell, who am I kidding?" It was huge! Now we were both ready.

Chance then braced himself firmly against me. Our bodies pressed against one another, my dark brown skin against his dark brown skin. My body screamed his name out loud and he answered. This was my fantasy, the love scene that had played over and over again inside my head for the past year. Chance was now my reality! He was all that I had known, and this was going to be my ultimate expression of love. This was to be my first time!

My clitoris thumped out a peculiar beat as I took the tip of his dick between my fingers and wedged it against the juicy entrance of my vagina. I was throbbing! I wanted it so bad, but I was so scared! Chance sensed my fear and paused a moment, looking deeply into my eyes through the constant downpour of rain. I kissed his lips and took the deepest breath of my life as he pushed himself inside me.

I then wrapped my legs around him as he picked me up, slowly stroking me back and forth. I put my arms around his neck as he held me up in the air. I squeezed his massive arms as they flexed. With his hard dick still inside me, he carried me into the house, grunting as he forcefully pushed the heavy glass door back open to make his way through the kitchen and over to the white cushioned wicker sofa in the sunroom that faced outward at the beach, where the storm pounded the foamy surf against shore.

Chance laid me down on the sofa and stepped out of his boxers, with his dick sharply at attention. I could still smell the sweet sea breeze mixing with the rain as it blew in through the open door. I could still hear the waves crashing outside almost in perfect time with the sound of my own beating heart, while *Joe* sang "*If I Was Yo' Man*" over the Bose Stereo System.

Chance kneeled down before me and kissed me. Then he moved down to my neck, my breast, and my stomach as he kissed my thighs and parted my legs. He slowly twirled his tongue around my clit again and again, until I came. I seemed almost instant! I began to moan out of control as he took his time and tasted every single drop of my love. Every little drip drop!

After what had to be two or three of the most intense orgasms known to man, Chance pulled himself up toward me at eye level and slowly worked his dick back inside me. It was so good that I could not help but dig my nails inside his him as he dug himself deeper inside me. I shuttered as he tapped what I guess was my "*G-Spot*"! Over and over and over again until I exploded! A loud scream of passion escaped from my lips as I convulsed in a sexual seizure.

Then, he put my legs up in the air and began to fuck me slowly, still taking his time. Pushing his dick all the way inside me then pulling it all the way out, teasing me with it. I was in the sweetest of agony and the river that flowed from inside me was his proof. I would have never imagined that I could feel so good. My heart began to race out of control and my pussy started to quiver in an unusually intense spasm as he began to pound me. I wanted to scream but I couldn't catch my breath!

Chance plunged and thrust himself inside me until he started to go into his own ecstatic spasm and then he squeezed me tightly and shouted out loud "Oh, Angell! Yes! Yes!"

releasing every little drop of passion he had inside.

Chance trembled as I touched his mocha colored skin. I could feel the goose bumps raise up on his body as he lay next to me. Then, he put his arms around me and held me close to his heart. I drifted peacefully off to sleep as he kissed my lips goodnight.

And then came the real drama!

CHAPTER 23

When I woke up the next morning it was still raining and the sky was a deep dark grey. It was about 8:30 and the house was dead silent. The rumble of approaching thunder and bright flashes of lightning filled the atmosphere and periodically broke through the quiet, as I looked out of Chance's bedroom window, where I had spent the night.

It was the most incredible night of my whole life. It was truly everything that I thought it would be and then some. I had waited twenty-nine years to share this most prized and sacred part of myself. And I must confess that it didn't quite happen the way that I thought I would. But it was still incredible, and still very much worth the wait.

I was floating on cloud-9 as I grabbed a sheet off of Chance's bed and wrapped it around myself. I opened the bedroom door and made my way to the bathroom to get showered.

After that, I hurried downstairs to look for Chance. I figured that he was probably down in the kitchen fixing breakfast or out on the back deck staring out at the ocean as he often did, but he wasn't in either place.

"Maybe he just went for a jog on the beach." I thought. But it was about to storm.

"So, why would he go running in the rain?"

I started to get nervous, but then I thought to myself "Girl, quit trippin'! The man probably just went down the street to the store." So I went to the front of the house to see if he might be coming down the street, but before I could get outside the door, I noticed that his keys were missing from the hook where he always kept them and his car was gone. Something was wrong!

I knew I was probably over reacting, but usually Chance never left the house without telling me. I had started to get a real uneasy feeling. Just then the doorbell rang.

So, I walked over and looked out of the window to see who was there. It was some chick, but I didn't recognize her face. "Maybe it was one of the neighbors." I thought as I opened the door.

"Hello. Is Evan home?" The girl said as I peeked out of the door.

"Evan? Oh, you mean Chance. He isn't here. Can I help you?" I responded, opening the door a wider to get a better look at who I was talking to.

The girl stood silently for a moment, just looking at me strangely. I started thinking that maybe she was one of Chance's ex-girlfriends who just dropped by to see him and found me there instead, but he never talked about anyone.

She stared at me like a deer caught in my headlights as a huge flash of lightning struck and the thunder rolled like the cadence from a bass drum.

The strange girl stood completely motionless, looking at me and through me at the same time. She all but hypnotized me with her deep-set hazel eyes.

She was beautiful, in a very hood sort of way. She kind of looked like a younger Vanessa Williams, but only way thicker. Her skin was a glowing honey brown. She had radiant straight white teeth and full luscious lips that almost pouted as she stared me down.

Her hair was long, flowing and freshly done, and the reddish dark chestnut color brought out the brown in her eyes.

The girl had a knock out body! She was short and curvy. Her cleavage peeked out from her hot pink *Baby Phat* haltered top, while the tight fitting Dolce & Gabana jeans she wore, snuggly hugged her round & shapely baby makin' hips. Everything about this bitch screamed GHETTO FABULOUS! So, what would she be doing here looking for Chance?

As she stepped a bit closer I could smell the Pear-Glaze Bath & Body fragrance she wore. I briefly hesitated. Something about her was strangely familiar but I couldn't pin point what it was.

I became uneasy and quickly stepped back.

"Well, Chance is not here, and I'm kinda busy, is there something that I can help you with?" I asked as I began growing more curious about what she wanted. We both stood quietly again for a second, just looking at each other. Then she spoke.

"You really don't know who I am, do you?" The sassy ghetto princess asked as she put one hand on her hip and cocked her head to the side.

"Excuse me!" I said, wondering what the hell she meant.

"Should I know you?" I responded.

"You mean you really have no idea who I am?" She asked again, as if she thought that I might be lying.

"Look, I have to go, okay? I'll tell Chance you stopped by, who ever you are." I said as I proceeded to shut the door. Cuz, this bitch was trippin'!

"Wait a minute!" She said as she pressed her hand up against the door. I instantly snapped into ghetto mode.

"Look, I told you, Chance wasn't here! What are you doin'?" I shouted as I snatched the door back open and raised my fist to start beatin' her ass. I was already pissed off at another high yellow heffa', so smackin' this one would have been just the stress reliever I needed.

"Wait! (She paused) "Chance and I use to live together" (She paused again) "We were engaged to be married" (She paused once more) "I'm the mother of his child. My name is Rayqelle"

I felt like I had just been kicked in the stomach by a pack mule. And then it dawned on me where I had seen her before and why she looked so familiar. She was the light skinned girl in the pictures that Chance had all over his bedroom dresser. That girl was his fiancé.

Then something else dawned on me. I knew this bitch from somewhere else beside those pictures. I had seen this girl before. Then it hit! The little light skinned guy in the hooded sweat shirt that had been following me around, scaring me out of my mind for the last couple of weeks was standing right in front of me. The times I had seen her before she was wearing boy clothes, but the eyes were unmistakable. The guy that had been stalking me was really a girl, and she was also Chance's baby-mama!

"I have known Chance for well over a year and he has never mentioned anything about you or any other bitch! And he sure as hell never mentioned anything about having a child! What kind of a game are you running?" I asked as I became infuriated.

"It's no game! Chance never knew that I was pregnant. (She paused) "We got separated before I could to tell him. It's the truth and I'm here to tell Chance today!" she said calmly with a relentless certainty in her voice that shook me to the core.

I was devastated! I didn't want to believe her but something told me that she was forreal. And my worst fears were realized when Chance came walking up behind me from the kitchen, unaware of what waited for him at the front door.

"Hey Angell, I just ran out to get a few things from the grocery store. Tonight I'm gonna make you a..." Chance froze dead in his tracks and stared at the strange woman as if he had seen a ghost, because in deed he had. The love of his life was not dead, but very much alive and standing right in front of him.

Unknown to me, Chance had a bit of a dark past. A few years ago he had been arrested and charged with murder. He was accused of the brutal slaying of Rayqelle's ex-college roommate (Iesha Ellis). But she was actually killed by Rayqelle's jealous ex-boyfriend, a small time hustla' from L.A. named Tico Vega.

The F.B.I. wanted to nail Tico in order to get to the major crime boss that he was working for. Rayqelle had a lot of information that the feds wanted really bad. So the state's Attorney General made a deal with her when she was in the hospital after being brutally attacked by Tico.

While she was hospitalized she had slipped into a drug-induced coma and was pronounced dead by the attending physician. But she was never really dead at all.

The F.B.I. told Rayqelle that If she would turn state's evidence and tell everything that she knew about Tico Vega and his organization, then disappear into the witness relocation program, the state would drop all charges against Chance and let him go free. Rayqelle had to be declared legally dead and never again have any kind of contact with Chance or anybody else that she knew.

So out of her unconditional love for him, she agreed to die, so that he could live. She gave her life in exchange for his.

Now, Rayqelle and I both stood in the doorway between heaven and hell, with each of our destinies placed squarely in the hands of fate and at *The Risk of Chance.*

I always love to hear from my readers and my fans! So, send me an email & let me know what you think>

koleblackwriter@yahoo.com

See you soon!

Here's a preview of the next
exciting novel by Kole Black>

"Chance Of The Game"

The tension in the car was thick enough to cut with a knife. Chance remained absolutely silent as we crossed MacArthur Causeway and headed on to I-395.

When we got to NW 14th street & 7th avenue, Chance pulled up and parked in front of what looked like an abandoned building that was all boarded up. He turned off his BMW and just sat quietly for a moment in deep thought.

"Shantess, sit here and don't move! I'll be right back. And keep the doors locked and windows up, and don't open 'em for anybody!" Chance commanded as he carefully got out of the car and shut the door. He was sexy as hell. I wanted to reach out and touch him. I wanted to comfort him. What I really wanted was to be the woman that her yearned for. But who was I to him besides Angell's little cousin, just another hoodrat from Liberty City. Chance just didn't know that I would have been anything that he wanted me to be. I had done everything that I could to show him, but all he could think about was trying to rescue that dope fiend skank that claimed to be the mother of his son.

This was the same bitch that had betrayed him with lies before.

"Chance! Wait! Where are you going? You can't just be roamin' around out here, these niggas will fuck you up! This ain't Cincinnati. This is the MIA, where mutha'fuckas come up M.I.A. Chance! Do you hear me? Where the fuck are you goin'?" I shouted as Chance ignored me and shut the door.

"Stay here!" Chance walked away and headed over to the side of the abandoned building and knocked on the door, but there was no answer, so he walked cautiously around to the back, where he disappeared from my line of sight.

Chance knocked on a partially boarded up window, but again there was no answer. And then he heard a metal click from behind him as he felt the cold steel from a gun barrel being pressed against the back of his head.

"Don't move mutha'fucka! Don't even breathe! 'Cuz as soon as you do, I'm gon' splatter yo' goddamn brains all over the side of this wall!" a man said calmly with a thick Haitian accent.

"You just made the biggest mistake of yo' life, nigga! But the good news is you won't be makin' no mo'! Now, turn yo' punk ass around, real slow!" The man with the Haitian voice said. Then he paused.

"Aw, Hell naw! Chance? Is that you? Man, what the hell you doin' in Overtown? Creepin' around out here in the dark like you the damn police! Don't 'chu know you almost got 'cho ass blasted?" It was Suede Le'joe, a nigga that Chance did business with when he first got to Miami.

This nigga was straight up hood, with a very short fuse and a deadly trigger finger that was itchy as hell. But oddly enough, in his own way, he had the greatest respect for Chance and proved it right then by sparing his life.

Because of Chance's reputation and their street and their street history together,

Suede had almost come to see Chance as more like a brother.

"What's up, Suede?" Chance said, looking him fearlessly in the eye, which said a lot. Suede was big & intimidating. He was 6'5 and 280 pounds of raw muscle, and his massive arms were almost completely covered by Haitian tats. He wore a full set of gold fronts in his mouth, and he had a very, very dark complexion. He was not the nigga you wanted to be caught alone by at night while in the back of an old abandoned building.

"So what are you doing here at this time of night? Don't tell me you're back in the game", Suede said as he reached into his pocket for a smoke.

"Ask me if I was ever out. This game is for life, once you're in it, ain't no gettin'' out, not really, no matter what you do. You know that, Suede." (Chance paused and breathed deep) "I'm here because I need yo' help. My baby's mama is missing, somebody kidnapped her, and I think they might be here in Overtown." Chance said as he looked around at the surrounding project low rises.

"Oh, word? That's fucked up! Do you know anything about who's got her?" Suede asked as he lit and puffed a Black.

"Yeah, some mutha'fucka named Vega, Tico Vega! He's a small time nigga from L.A." (Chance paused) "He's also got my son" Chance responded as he leaned against the crumbling brick wall.

"I guess this Tico Vega nigga don't know who the fuck you really are" Suede said as he stared at the fiery tip of his Black n' Mild.

"No, and neither does anybody else." Chance replied as he looked out of over the filthy streets of Overtown with his mind focused on first getting his son back, and then, getting revenge on Tico Vega.

To order this & other novels by Kole Black, just go to>

WWW.SPAULDENPUBLISHING.COM